BOOKS BY ROBERT L. FISH

RUB-A-DUB-DUB

WHIRLIGIG

WITH MALICE TOWARD ALL *(a Mystery Writers of
America Anthology)*

THE MURDER LEAGUE

THE HOCHMANN MINIATURES

THE INCREDIBLE SCHLOCK HOMES

THE TRIALS OF O'BRIEN

THE ASSASSINATION BUREAU, LTD. *(Completion of an
unfinished work by Jack London)*

Captain José Da Silva novels:

THE GREEN HELL TREASURE

THE XAVIER AFFAIR

THE BRIDGE THAT WENT NOWHERE

ALWAYS KILL A STRANGER

BRAZILIAN SLEIGH RIDE

THE DIAMOND BUBBLE

THE SHRUNKEN HEAD

ISLE OF THE SNAKES

THE FUGITIVE *(winner of the Mystery Writers of
America Edgar Award)*

Under the Pseudonym of Robert L. Pike:

POLICE BLOTTER

THE QUARRY

MUTE WITNESS

REARDON

RUB-A-DUB-DUB

AN INNER SANCTUM MYSTERY
BY

Robert L. Fish

SIMON AND SCHUSTER · NEW YORK

COPYRIGHT © 1971 BY ROBERT L. FISH
PUBLISHED BY SIMON AND SCHUSTER
ROCKEFELLER CENTER, 630 FIFTH AVENUE
NEW YORK, NEW YORK 10020

FIRST PRINTING
SBN 671-20895-0
LIBRARY OF CONGRESS CATALOG CARD NUMBER:
    78-154065
MANUFACTURED IN THE UNITED STATES OF AMERICA
BY THE BOOK PRESS, NEW YORK

This Book Is Dedicated

to

BOB AND PAT MILLS

RUB-A-DUB-DUB

1

Captain Charles Everton Manley-Norville, master of the luxury liner the S.S. *Sunderland* out of Southampton, stood on the bridge of his pride and joy and smiled mechanically down on the bobbing heads of passengers clambering bravely up the sharply tilted gangplank to disappear gratefully into the purser's square on the Main Deck. Behind the captain, his youngish executive officer leaned casually on the polished railing, awaiting the time to call the idling tugs into action to pull them into the Solent, wondering what was in store for lunch and if any single girls with decent shapes and indecent morals might be included in the passenger list for the cruise. Beyond him, the stained red brick and chimney pots of Southampton appeared lilliputian from the august height of the liner's bridge.

The dock below was strewn with friends and relatives screaming to the travelers above; those on deck screamed back. Nobody could understand a word, but then, nobody was truly expected to. At the stern of the ship, using a second gangplank leading to the open portion of a lower deck, porters trundled back and forth, handing luggage with the insouciance and the

it's-not-my-bloody-luggage-it-belongs-to-them-rich-baskits attitude
of porters the world over, throwing the bags at the room stewards as if testing their bowling ability. On the deck children
dashed back and forth, adding their shrill cries to the cacophony
and knocking down other children while pursued by parents,
nannys and deck stewards. The tall yard cranes, finished with
their loading tasks, waited patiently like so many gigantic fla-
mingos; their operators, perched midway up the monsters, blew
their horns every few minutes for no reason whatsoever. With a
good half hour yet until the actual sailing, the lineup for com-
plaints had already formed in the purser's square, interfering with
incoming traffic and compounding the general confusion. Unin-
telligible noises issued echoingly from loudspeakers mounted
haphazardly about the ship; they sounded quite official and even
dire. The ship's whistle, as if to clear its throat in order to be
prepared for any contingency, blasted at irregular intervals.

It was, in fine, a typical departure of a typical passenger ocean
liner off on a cruise.

Captain Manley-Norville appeared quite deaf to the racket
that rose from both above and below him. The captain was a
large, florid, rather handsome man, with a properly corseted
figure encased in a properly blue-and-gold uniform, heavily
striped at the cuffs. He had a thick mane of gray hair, piercing
gray eyes beneath bushy eyebrows, and a manner that could be
brusque or breezy as the occasion demanded. His smile, as he
stood watching the animals herded two by two into his ark, remained a fixed, humorless affair. Captain Manley-Norville had
seen the same scene too many times to exhibit enthusiasm.

But then, suddenly, his smile widened into a genuine expression of pleasure. His eye had caught and held three elderly gentlemen laboriously mounting the shaky gangplank. The trio
were celebrities of the moment, widely publicized in the press,
and Captain Manley-Norville liked nothing better than having
celebrities aboard his ship, particularly if they were aging gentle-

men in their seventies who would leave the stewardesses alone, not play Beatle records at three in the morning and in general cause no disturbance save, possibly, to the ship's surgeon. It was something, unfortunately, that could not always be said for young Brazilian millionaires, American television stars, French actresses or oversexed divorcées.

Over the years, Captain Charles Everton Manley-Norville had reached his high rank of authority because of his great discernment, his almost infallible judgment, and his extraordinarily sharp eye for hanky-panky in any form among either crew or passengers. He was not, however, prescient: the future did not reveal itself to him. Nor, of course, could he read minds. It is therefore possible to forgive him for having widened his smile at sight of the three, for he had nothing more to go on than their general appearance of harmlessness and the stories the press had so recently printed about them. With more basis for judgment, his smile most certainly would have been a grimace of deep pain; assuredly he would have exercised his authority to have the master-at-arms ban the three from the ship or possibly even drop them overboard; or, failing these, the captain might well have ordered the S.S. *Sunderland* into midstream and there, personally, scuttled her. In the long run it might well have saved him grief.

Of course, had the captain taken any of these eminently sensible precautionary measures, our three elderly gentlemen would not have been able to enjoy the holiday cruise for which they had planned and anticipated so many months. And in that case —more importantly—we should not have had our story.

But he didn't, so they did, and we have. . . .

Leading the oddly paired (in any combination) trio up the swaying, slightly frightening gangplank was William (Billy-boy to his friends) Carruthers. He was a rotund, cherubic-looking man with exceedingly bright china-blue eyes set in a round face framed beneath a halo of pure white hair. He might well have posed for Missionary-of-the-Week in the *Christian Advocate*, or portrayed the part of an American senator in the cinema. He was dressed in a lightweight suit that was the only lightweight thing about him; it was faintly ecru in color—or possibly light mustard—and it did nothing to hide his portliness although it seemed to emphasize his innocence, since no villain would have been caught dead in it. He appeared the type to whom perfect strangers might well turn to ask the holding of wager stakes. He mounted the steps of the gangplank, taking them in dignified pace and smiling down at them pleasantly, as if counting them for some obscure reason of his own; then he glanced up as he approached the top, serene in his knowledge that he had acted the role of elderly-man-mounting-gangplank to perfection.

Behind him came Timothy Briggs, a tiny mite of a man with spikes of iron-gray hair standing out rebelliously from his tiny head. His little face was well seamed with wrinkles, but the sharpness of his small dark eyes might have warned the wary not to underestimate him. Tim Briggs was originally from Willington Quay on Tyneside and suspiciously required proof of all things. Besides, his experiences of late had taught him nothing if not caution of his fellowman, particularly if his fellowman happened to be a barrister and especially if that barrister happened to be named Pugh. Briggs had the general appearance of a sedately clad toy on an overwound spring, barely being held back from shoving Billy-boy Carruthers to one side and dashing up the remaining steps, either as a release for an excess of energy not to be denied or because he could not be sure the unstable gangplank would hold until he had made it safely to the top.

Clifford Simpson brought up the rear of the triumvirate. He was a gangling beanpole of a man, an unfolded ruler, roughly the height of his two friends placed one upon the other. He had a perpetual look of mild curiosity upon his long, thoughtful face, as if wondering what foible life could next produce but sure that it would be interesting. He had light-brown hair, little touched by age, although an occasional glimpse of pink scalp could be seen peeking through. His eyes were light green, a trifle hooded and always inquisitive. He was dressed in his usual tweeds, and his ever-present (when he could afford them) Corona cigar was locked between his well-fitting plates. He took the steps calmly, as he did everything else, although the unconsciously excessive movement of elbow and knee, Ichabod Crane style, made it appear he was taking them two at a time when, in fact, he was not.

The three made it to the purser's square on the Main Deck in one piece and paused to take stock of their surroundings. The racket about them was deafening, but it seemed to do nothing to dampen their spirits. The purser, casting his eyes about desperately in an attempt to avoid the complaint of the young American woman who had him by the collar, used their arrival as a welcome excuse to tear himself loose and hustle to their side, smiling brightly.

"Mr. Carruthers! Mr. Briggs! Mr. Simpson! Welcome aboard the S.S. *Sunderland!* I'd have recognized you from your pictures in a minute! A pleasure to have you traveling with us! Everything has been handled. Your luggage is in your stateroom— Number 45 on A Deck. And your keys—your keys!" He swung in the direction of the desk, babbling over his shoulder. "I'll get you your keys! One for each of you!"

Briggs frowned. Oddly enough, despite the fact that he had written scores of stories in which ships played a part, it was his first time on one, but he still wanted all protocol clear in his mind. He turned to Carruthers, speaking out of the corner of his mouth.

"Who's old Henry Helpful?"

While Carruthers had not traveled as a passenger for many years, his memory was infallible.

"That's the purser."

"And how much does *he* get tipped?"

"He doesn't," Carruthers said calmly, and then added in the interests of complete truth, "of course, he's about the only one on board who doesn't, I believe." He nodded his thanks to the uniformed figure, accepted the handful of keys, smiled a pleasant dismissal and then looked at his companions. "Well? Anyone for a quick wash? The loo? Or shall we watch our departure from the Promenade Deck?"

"We watch, of course!" Briggs said firmly. "I've never seen one, you know. And besides—at these prices?"

"We watch," Simpson agreed. "It's been years since I've been on a ship, you know—and then it was only an old army transport down to Gibraltar, in '15, I believe. . . ."

Carruthers, nothing loath, nodded his agreement, and the three moved in the direction of the elevator that served the various decks. One quick study of its size—which would have scarcely stood Billy-boy's girth let alone Simpson's height—and they forewent the mechanism, marching instead up the center stairway leading from the purser's square to the upper reaches of the ship. A turn in the steps and they had disappeared.

The irate young woman who had been abandoned by the purser captured him again before he could find a new excuse. Her voice, when she spoke, was more curious than angry.

"And just who are Papa Bear, Mama Bear, and Baby Bear? To get the red carpet rolled out for them, I mean?"

Fortunately the purser had traveled with colonials before and understood the intricacies of their language.

"They, Madam," he said with national pride ringing in his voice, "are the founding members of the Mystery Authors Club of Great Britain. Of course," he added a bit sadly, "they haven't any of them written anything for some thirty or forty years, but —" his voice rose again, undeterred "—at one time they were the most famous writers in England. A long time ago, it's true, but still . . . "

"And they're still big shots? What was the last thing they wrote? *Fanny Hill?*"

"No, Madam," said the purser, a bit stiffly. "That was John Cleland. They're not now famous for writing; they happen to be this year's winners of the J.G.L.H.N.M.S. award."

The young lady stared at him: "The who's what?"

The purser took a deep breath. The woman was after all, a foreigner and really not to be blamed for her ignorance. Besides, as long as they remained on other subjects, the young lady's complaint was—albeit temporarily—shelved, although he had a sad feeling that it wouldn't be shelved for long. There was something in her eye to make him believe it.

"The Jarvis-Greater-Love-Hath-No-Man-Society award, Mrs. Carpenter," he explained, trying to sound genial. "It is given each year to a person or persons whose personal sacrifice in the interests of a fellowman demonstrates a loyalty to the principles of friendship above and beyond the call of—" He seemed to realize he was sounding a bit like a recruiting poster and also that he was losing the attention of his audience. "That is—ah— well, friendship, you know. Yes. Yes, indeed. It—the award, that is—amounts to a matter of twenty thousand quid. Pounds, that is, ma'am."

The wavering attention of the young woman returned instantly.

"Twenty thousand pounds? You did say twenty thousand pounds?" Mrs. Carpenter's hidden antennae had begun to rotate, picking up signals. "What on earth did the old—I mean, what did they ever do to earn it?"

The purser was pleased to be able to furnish the details. After all, the press had printed little else for several weeks.

"Well, ma'am, one of them—Mr. Simpson, the tall one—was accused of murder, and his two friends sacrificed everything they had to hire England's leading barrister—lawyer to you, ma'am —Sir Percival Pugh, to save him. Sir Percival is famous for his exorbitant fees, but Mr. Briggs and Mr. Carruthers did not hesitate. They sold their meager possessions, spent the last of their small savings, borrowed extensively—" He saw he was in danger of losing his audience a second time and hurried to a conclusion. "Still," he ended, "they did win the award, and twenty thousand pounds is a lot of money."

"Over forty grand? Yes," Mrs. Carpenter agreed. "I wouldn't be the one to call it cheese." She frowned in deep thought for several moments and then, almost reluctantly, returned to the original purpose of her being there. "Now, Buster, about that midget broom closet you put me and my husband in . . . "

The three founding members of the Mystery Writers Club— and, although the purser was unaware of it, the Murder League as well—pushed through the heavy doors to the Promenade Deck and wandered to the rail. The decibel volume of parting had risen considerably; the loudspeakers were now exhorting those who should be ashore to get cracking, but they seemed to be doing so in some foreign language. It was a warm day and a faint sheen of perspiration beaded the brow of Mr. Carruthers; he attempted to get some relief from the breeze generated by several hundreds of frantically waving handkerchiefs, but it was insufficient. He patted his brow with his own and returned it neatly to his sleeve. Tim Briggs saw the gesture and glanced about almost truculently.

"No deck chairs?"

There were, in fact, deck chairs, but they were piled against the outer wall of the main salon, awaiting the ship's departure before being set out and assigned, for a fee, by the deck steward. Mr. Carruthers was familiar with this procedure, but he had never clearly understood the reason for it. Mr. Briggs, having never sailed on a cruise ship before, was not familiar with this form of piracy on the high seas, but he would have opposed it on general principles. If Mr. Simpson had ever known the rules and regulations governing deck chairs, he had long since forgotten them. Being the tallest, he therefore moved to one of the piles and handed down three of the complicated wooden puzzles. Briggs, oddly enough, managed to untangle them in record time; he snapped them into a semblance of a seating arrangement and spread them about. The three dropped into the chairs with sighs of relief.

The first thing that happened was that a small boy, screaming imprecations at his nursemaid and running without watching traffic, sprawled over Briggs and as a result was captured and led back by the ear to incarceration. He managed to squirm about long enough to treat the three to a most reproachful glance.

The second thing that happened—almost as quickly—was the appearance of the deck steward. His shocked look seemed to say that while he knew iconoclasm and revolution were the order of the day, still, there were limits.

"'Ere, now!" he said sternly. "Yer can't open deck chairs before the ship sails! And as a matter o' fact, yer can't open 'em at all, see? That's *me* job! And anyways, them chairs is to be rented; they ain't for free!"

Briggs leaned back, considering the white-jacketed man with scorn.

"Rubbish!" he said in a tone of voice that closed the matter for all time, at least as far as he was concerned. "Are you seriously suggesting that after buying and paying a bloody fortune for transport on a ship, one is expected to stand all the way?"

"On my trip to Gibraltar—it was in '15, you know—I don't recall paying for deck chairs," Simpson said reflectively. "In fact, I'm sure I didn't. I don't think any of us did." He frowned. "In fact, I'm not even sure we had deck chairs. It was an army transport, you see," he adding, looking up helpfully.

"Well, this ain't '15, whatever that is, and this ain't no army transport, gents—"

"My dear man," Carruthers interrupted with a bright smile.

"If I might cut in for a moment, possibly you could answer a question. My friends and I are unaccustomed, of late, to shipboard travel, and it is possible that on rare occasion we may do something gauche. If so, we are more to be pitied than censured. However, my question is this—" His hand disappeared into a pocket to emerge with a huge roll; a five-pound note graced the outside. "Is it customary to tip at the start of a voyage, or at its termination?"

The steward's eyes widened incredulously at the sight. He swallowed.

"Well—sir—some passengers does it one way, and some does the other. Yer can do it either way . . . "

"Oh, ah? Thank you. I shall remember that." The roll was held contemplatively. Billy-boy Carruthers brought his eyes up to consider the steward in kindly fashion. "Oh, yes," he went on, in the manner of one suddenly remembering something, "I wonder if you could be so kind as to bring myself and my friends a bit of something from the bar? A touch of brandy, shall we say —to give an inner balance to the temperature of the day?"

The steward's eyes followed the gently waving roll of money like a cobra responding to a properly played reed instrument.

"The bar ain't open in port, sir. The law, yer know."

"But surely one could arrange a pot of tea?" Carruthers smiled at him gently. "And in the tea one might find—might just find, that is—something a bit stronger than tea? I'm sure that a steward of your ingenuity—as witness the speed with which you discovered our transgression regarding the deck chairs—must be able to procure the cooperation of a fellow member of the shipboard proletariat. Like one of the bartenders, for example."

The steward shook his head unhappily. "Honest, gents. It really can't be done . . . "

"Come, come!" Simpson said sternly, sitting a bit more erect and fixing the steward with his eye. "Is this the spirit that carried Nelson to victory at Toulon—I believe it was Toulon—and at Trafalgar? I'm sure it was Trafalgar. At any rate, is this—?"

"This 'It really can't be done,'" Briggs interrupted. "Is this the sort of attitude that allowed Raleigh to destroy the Spanish Armada?"

"I was going to come to Raleigh," Simpson said to his smaller companion chidingly and turned back to the steward. "Well, enough of examples; history fairly reeks of them. At any rate, if these changes are now part of the lore of the British sailing man, all I can say is he's certainly gone downhill over the years. Back in '15—"

Billy-boy Carruthers raised a hand to give Simpson pause; he seemed surprised to find it was the hand holding the bulky roll. He slipped it into his pocket and smiled at the steward.

"It wouldn't have to be French brandy. Or, actually, brandy at all. I can see your problem, and I sympathize. Champagne would do nicely, if it had to . . . "

The steward shook his head as if to clear it of cobwebs. "Champagne? I'll see what I can do for yer gents, sir," he said, and managed his escape.

Briggs frowned. "I hope those aren't all five-pound notes in that bundle, Billy-boy. I know we're on board ship with a bunch of so-called millionaires and all that, but even so. In fact, even single quids in a roll like that . . . "

Carruthers looked at him reproachfully.

"Really, Tim! This is what you conceived yourself in *Monte Carlo Mayhem*. Don't you recall Sir Harry Melton and how he impressed the fair Lady Wallingford with his famous stack of money?"

"Oh, ah!" Briggs said, ashamed both of his lack of memory and his suggestion that Billy-boy would have been foolish enough to carry around cash in that quantity. "Of course! Sixteen-pound rag bond, isn't it? Almost the same texture and feel as the real stuff."

"Exactly," Carruthers said, and smiled his forgiveness. "Cut with a razor and a straightedge, of course. Uneven edges would be fatal." His glance rose and his beaming smile faded a trifle, becoming a bit set. "Well, well, well!" he continued softly. "A small world! Look who we just bought for a shipmate . . . !"

His two companions swung about in their deck chairs to see what had caused the sudden change on Billy-boy's usually cherubic face. Walking down the Promenade Deck with the air of a man who has just bought the ship and was having difficulty deciding which improvements he would inaugurate first, was none other than that famous brain, knight of the realm, and eminent barrister Sir Percival Pugh!

Briggs was the first to speak, and his words revealed that his memory, while possibly a bit weak where Sir Harry Melton and Lady Wallingford were concerned, was quite up to date on Sir Percival Pugh.

"Twister!" he said bitterly. "What's he doing on this ship?"

"Come, now, Tim," Simpson said chidingly. "He did save my life, you know."

"He didn't mind charging for it, either," Briggs retorted hotly.

"And as for his being aboard, it *is* a cruise that's open to the public," Carruthers reminded him.

"Then they should be more careful who they include in the public!" He stared with cold eyes as Sir Percival passed them, giving the three a friendly smile and a pleasant nod in turn.

"Well, now," Carruthers said with logic, "you're scarcely being fair. If he hadn't charged us such an exorbitant fee, we'd never have won that alphabetical award, you know."

But Timothy Briggs of Tyneside was not to be placated.

"My advice to you, Billy-boy," he said direly, "is that you replace that fiver on top of that fake roll of money. Old Pugh wouldn't stop at fiddling *that* off you if he had half a chance!"

It is true that Sir Percival had a reputation for loving money, and he would have been the first to confirm the truth of that statement. Nor did he see the slightest thing wrong with loving money. On the other hand, there was no doubt that he earned the money he received, being the finest counsel one could have at his side in time of trouble. Sir Percival had never lost a case in his life, and he had no intention of ever doing so, although—as stated—any prospective client seeking his succor was well-advised to have more than a widow's pittance in his pocket.

It was therefore that—despite the pleasant smile and friendly nod he had bestowed on the founding members of the Mystery Authors Club and the ex-members of the now defunct Murder League—there was a touch of sadness in his soul as he continued down the deck. Twenty thousand pounds were in the possession of the three old men, and even though Sir Percival was on holiday, he could see no reason why he should not combine business with pleasure and separate them from at least a portion of it. He sighed mightily and put the thought away as being unproductive. Even knowing the trio for what they were, Sir Percival could not imagine how even those three could get into enough trouble aboard a ship to warrant their requiring—or asking for—his assistance.

Odd as it may seem to those familiar with his giant intellect, Sir Percival Pugh was, possibly for the first time in his long and distinguished career, quite wrong. . . .

2

"Vorny nounand nucks," said Mrs. Carpenter. She was sitting in a sheer and attractive dressing gown before the mirrored dressing table in their now-vastly-improved stateroom, putting her hair up and speaking through a mouthful of hairpins. It was obvious from the luxury of their accommodations that Mrs. Carpenter had prevailed upon the purser in one manner or another, of which she had many. Her steely eyes watched herself in the mirror carefully, as if to make sure her image didn't do anything it shouldn't.

Mr. Carpenter shoved his head from the bathroom. He was a small, thin, dapper man, a trifle smaller than his wife, with small, sharp eyes, ears that stuck from his head at ninety-degree angles, patent-leather hair, and a hairline mustache which, at the moment, he was attempting to shave around. He held the razor poised above the billows of lather on his sunken cheeks, staring at his wife in bewilderment.

"What did you say, sweets?"

"I said, forty thousand bucks. Take the soap out of your ears," Mrs. Carpenter said in an unkindly fashion. She checked her appearance in the mirror and found it properly satisfying—for despite the hard look about her mouth that she was not even aware of, Mrs. Carpenter was a good-looking woman in the final lap of her twenties, with an excellent figure and a good complexion. She swung about on the small plastic seat, pulling her dressing gown about her, eyeing her husband coldly. "Forty grand, that's what I said—if a month in Europe made you forget the English language altogether."

"Oh."

Mr. Carpenter disappeared into the bathroom again; there were several moments of silence before he returned to the stateroom proper, wiping the excess lather from his thin face with a towel. He passed a hand over his cheeks, smiling at their smoothness, tossed the towel carelessly behind him into the bathroom and turned to the tall dresser in one corner, humming slightly to himself. The sound seemed to annoy his spouse.

"Did you hear what I said, Max?"

"I heard you, sweets. A couple characters got the luck of a guy with a bicycle in a red-light district with everybody else walking. So?"

"So?" Mrs. Carpenter had switched from her hair to her nails; she looked up from her new task with a look of disgust. "You got to be getting old, Max! I said forty grand! If we can't take a chunk of that much dough away from three old cockers the age of my grandfather, we ought to hang up! We ought to switch over to peddling oil stocks in the lobby of the Shamrock in Texas, or selling gold bricks in front of the New York Stock Exchange!"

"As I recall your old grandfather," Max Carpenter said absently, searching through a drawer for a shirt, "you couldn't talk that old tightwad out of a bad cold."

"I said the *age* of my grandfather, stupid!" Mrs. Carpenter blew on her nails, studied them critically and put away her manicure set. She reached for her makeup kit, her dressing gown gaping alarmingly. She pulled it together absently and reached for her rouge. "These three sad sacks have to be tea on toast—"

"Jam on toast, sweets," Max said, and pulled a proper-looking shirt free. "That's the way they say it."

"Gravy, then. They look like they should have brought along a baby-sitter, only they forgot." With that much money in the offing, Mrs. Carpenter wasn't in the mood, at the moment, to argue.

Mr. Max Carpenter fumbled with shirt studs. Actually, he didn't mind dressing for dinner; in a white formal jacket he looked more distinguished than in his usual pullover and slacks; in addition, his patent-leather shoes had three-inch lifts which brought him up to his wife's height, if no higher.

"All right, Mazie. What do you suggest?"

"Well," Mazie Carpenter said, giving the matter serious thought, "cards is what I suggest." She put down the rouge and picked up the lipstick. "I doubt if we could get any of them interested in annuities at their age, and mining stocks are a little cornball, even in England—or on a limey boat, which is the same thing. Besides, they don't look like they'd be around to clip very many coupons, even if somebody ever discovered gold in one of those mines."

"True," said Mr. Carpenter, knotting his bow tie. He tugged it into line and examined it from several angles. As always, it was perfect. He grinned knowingly at himself in the mirror and gave himself a wink for good measure. "Especially since they don't exist."

He tucked his shirttails in place, snapped his suspenders around his thin shoulders and reached for his cummerbund. He wound it about his waist expertly with the skill of a flamenco dancer, tucked the end in decisively, and then flexed his thin but strong fingers with the agility and rippling motion of the professional card manipulator. Suddenly he frowned. He had seen a fly, roughly the size of a pterodactyl, in the ointment.

"But, Mazie, sweets—what if they don't play cards?"

"Then I'll teach 'em," Mrs. Carpenter said with finality and began to apply her lipstick.

The three elderly gentlemen to whom the Carpenters, Max and Mazie, were at that moment referring were also—oddly enough—discussing the matter of money. They had enjoyed an early meal, although the headwaiter had been disposed to be a bit sticky about the question of formal costume until Mr. Carruthers inadvertently transferred his funds from one pocket to another, being rather careless enough to be seen in the act. After that things went swimmingly. They were now ensconced at a corner table in the bar just outside the main salon, seated in deep leather chairs, where they somehow felt akin to the corner of the Mystery Authors Club which they had long since taken over as their own. True, the wide window of the ship's bar gave view at the moment to a stunningly beautiful sunset rather than the staid office building that faced them in London, but this was only to the good. Before them a quite creditable brandy stood in properly shaped glasses; a bottle of excellent champagne nestled in an ice bucket at their side.

"I will admit," Briggs said grudgingly, "that the drinks aboard this ship are reasonably priced. I'd be lying if I denied that. But, even so, it's a rather boring way to spend money."

Simpson frowned at him in alarm, his eyebrows rising to join his low hairline. "On drinks?"

"No, no! I mean this travel thing. I mean this sailing pointlessly from here to there. After all, when this cruise bit is over, where will we be? Back in Southampton. We were there just a day ago." He shifted himself further back in his chair, bringing his feet further from the floor. "Why leave in the first place?"

Carruthers looked at him with such a glance of hidden amusement that Briggs felt called upon to explain.

"What I mean is, there isn't a thing to *do* on this ship!"

Simpson carefully clipped the tip from a Corona and nodded his head; with his thinness and excessive height he looked something like a stork bobbing for minnows.

"Actually," he said in a thoughtful voice, "I must agree with Tim." He took time to light his cigar and puff it into activity and then continued. "Possibly we might better have saved the money and invested it with the rest."

"Come, come, lads!" Mr. Carruthers appeared disappointed with his friends. "Less than six months ago we all agreed that ten thousand pounds, judiciously invested—as we must all admit the money has been invested—would provide ample funds in dividends for our simple needs. The balance we agreed to splurge. On shipboard travel, for one." He frowned at them a bit curiously. "So why this sudden parsimony?"

"It isn't parsimony," Briggs protested. "It's just—well, to be blunt, it was a lot more fun making money than it is spending it. At least aboard this ship," he added stubbornly.

"The truth is, we did have fun those three months with the Murder League," Simpson said reflectively. He removed his cigar from his lips and smiled in an embarrassed fashion, looking at the others. "I say! You don't suppose that even aboard this ship—?"

Carruthers' eyebrows rose in shock. "Cliff!"

"Oh, I don't mean killing people," Simpson said hastily and then added, "although I'm sure there are many aboard who would be as equally deserving as our past victims. I just thought—"

"He's right," Briggs said positively. "What harm could there be in some innocent fun, just to pass the time? And pick up a quid or two on the side? Say in fixing the afternoon Bingo? It wouldn't be hard at all." He leaned forward as his mind set the scene. "Those little balls with the numbers on them; I know where the library steward keeps them. I was chatting with him this morning—bloody little else to do—and I noticed where he keeps the games and things locked up. A cupboard and a drawer, and I could open either one of them with a toothpick."

"There will be none of that!" Carruthers said, truly scandalized. "You know we've given up anything even the slightest bit dishonest! I thought that was abundantly clear!"

"What about the ship's pool?" Simpson said, studying the end of his cigar rather than contemplating the look in Billy-boy's eye. "As I recall, in your book *Pigalle Passion*—which, if I never mentioned it before, I thought excellent—you had a character named Left-Bank Louis who was able to palm a slip of paper so well that at a crucial moment in the plot, he couldn't find it himself. I always thought that a beautiful thought, but what I'm getting at is that I also seem to remember your practicing the art for hour after hour. . . ."

Carruthers felt his face getting red.

"That was a long time ago," he said stiffly, "and arthritis has scarcely aided any manual dexterity I had forty years ago. Besides, we've given up anything even the slightest bit shady. I thought that was agreed upon."

"But why?" Briggs wailed.

"For many reasons, but I'll give you another. Do you know," Carruthers said, dropping his voice, leaning forward and even putting aside his brandy glass momentarily to lend emphasis to his words, "that an American writer got hold of our adventures of this past year and wrote them up? They were published, all right—he even called the book *The Murder League*—but one of the book clubs devoted entirely to detective fiction refused to reprint the thing because the three of us were such naughty people? As a result, this writer—a rather good one, I understand—lost a valuable sale. Now, certainly we wouldn't want this to happen to a person in our field of endeavor—or at least our ex-field—would we?" He leaned back, his point, he was sure, proven.

"Seems to me the bloody American writer brought it on himself," Briggs said cruelly. "What bloody business did he have poking his nose into our affairs in the first place? And taking our name—that's plagiarism and actionable, I wouldn't be surprised."

"I'm not sure about the actionable part of a title, since it can't be copyrighted," Simpson said, "but Briggs still has a point." He rolled his cigar in his fingers, his eyes still avoiding Carruthers' face. "We all took our chances; this writer took his. He just got caught telling the truth. Can't be too bright for a fiction writer is all I can say."

"Can't be too bright, period!" Briggs said harshly.

"Enough!" Carruthers' tone carried finality. He rose to his feet majestically. "Fiddling is out. I don't even intend to discuss it further. I believe I saw someone using a backgammon set in the library not long ago. If you must have excitement, try that." He completed his brandy and turned the glass upside down to make sure he had left nothing for the bar steward. "I'm off to bed. Anyone joining me?"

"Later," Briggs said morosely and hunched down in his chair. "I'm not sleepy. I may do cat's cradles for an hour or so, if my aging heart can stand the excitement."

"I think I'll take a few turns about the deck before turning in," Simpson said. "Finish my cigar, so to speak. Ta-ta."

"Ta," said Carruthers, and trudged from the room.

There was a moment's silence, and then, "They're setting up for the horse races in the main lounge," Briggs said, his voice low and his eye cocked warily on the heavy door swinging shut behind their portly companion. Satisfied, he turned, an air of secrecy about him, looking Simpson squarely in the eye. "How about it, Cliff?"

Simpson returned the steady glance. "Are you suggesting—?"

"I just thought the two of us might care to take a flyer."

There were several moments of silence as Simpson considered the proposition. His eyes came up to the small wizened face beside him; they then moved to the closed door to make sure Billy-boy Carruthers had, indeed, actually disappeared. A faint smile appeared on his lips.

"I gather it's the sort of flyer one wouldn't care to make alone?"

"You gather correctly."

"Well, in that case, I believe I would. A lovely thing, the sport of kings," he said, and drained the last of the champagne.

The chairs had been cleared back from the edges of the dance floor of the Main Salon to allow room for a long strip of green felt that served as the track for the traditional shipboard game. Painfully thin wooden horses, each with a number painted brightly on its side, stood waiting patiently at the starting line. Bellboys in uniform shifted weight from foot to foot, ready to move the horses on orders. The library steward, in charge of games, felt the salon had filled with sufficient aficionados. He glanced over at the Captain sitting calmly to one side, saw nothing in the expressionless visage to say him yea or nay and hammered on the table for silence.

"Ladies and gentlemen. Your attention please."

There was the usual shuffling of feet and momentary outbreak of coughing and sneezing at announcements of this sort, but in a few moments they had subsided. The library steward took a deep breath.

"For those here who have not previously played horse racing," he intoned, "please allow me to explain the track rules. Those to whom this is old hat, please bear with me. There are six horses, one for each number on a dice. They advance along the strip from square to square in accordance with the number of times their number comes up on the three dice in this small cage. The cage is twirled in each game by a different volunteer from among the passengers—yourselves, that is. This, the first race, is a steeplechase; that is, a barrier has been set four squares

31

from the end. To hurtle this barrier, one must wait for a double in the throw of the dice. One must also await a double in order to go from the final square to the winner's circle."

He paused a moment as if to be sure his audience had not fallen asleep, cleared his throat apologetically and tried not to sound like a man repeating himself for approximately the four-thousandth time.

"As is customary at the Sunderland Track, the first and last races of the day are played for double the normal stakes. Anyone playing the game may purchase as many tickets on each horse as he or she chooses. Tickets for the other races are priced at ten shillings each; for the first and final games, at one pound. Is it all clear? Any questions? Good-o, then! The pari-mutuel windows are open!"

He smiled brightly at the group, although, if the truth were known, the library steward was heartily sick of having to run the games aboard ship. He had taken the position of library steward fifteen years earlier because he had a strong feeling—after seeing the intricately engraved spines and spotted brown leaves of the books locked up there—that few people would be curling up in a chair with Thackeray or Oliver Goldsmith. He had anticipated ample time for a certain pretty stewardess on C Deck; and then they had saddled him with the blasted games. The stewardess had long since married the owner of a landside pub. He watched the tickets being grabbed up like packets of gaspers back in '48 and sighed prodigiously. He caught the Captain's eye upon him and managed to turn the sigh into a delighted smile, no easy trick.

"You buy the tickets," Briggs said, sotto voce. "Number four. Get enough of them. I have a hunch it may win."

Simpson grinned at him.

"I'm quite sure you have," he said and wandered over to the table where the tickets were being dispensed by a very pretty girl. When his turn came he brought forth a goodly sum of pounds and exchanged them for an equal number of blue tickets. Turning, he bumped squarely into Captain Manley-Norville.

"Ah, Mr. Simpson." The master's eyes caught sight of the number of tickets in the other's hand. His gray eyes twinkled beneath their bushy brows. "I see you have a tip from the stable, eh? Number four, eh?"

Simpson smiled a ghastly smile. "Just a hunch, Captain."

"Well, sometimes they're almost as good as a shot of stimulant, especially with wooden horses. But I'm afraid we're holding up traffic." The Captain smiled. "In fact, I think I'll go along with you on number four, but only for one ticket. No J.G.L. etcetera awards for shipboard captains, you know."

He turned back to the table, allowing Simpson to escape, sweating slightly despite the air conditioning. The commerce of ticket selling continued for several minutes more and then dropped off. The box with the money was snapped shut; the library steward moved to the fore again, forcing bonhomie into his voice.

"Are we ready? Good-O! And a volunteer? Ah, fine! Mr. Briggs! How have you been? You understand your task? You merely twirl this little cage, and then when I read off the numbers on the dice, you verify my reading. In this way—" He chuckled. "Well, there'll be no doping of horses on *this ship*— I mean, this track—heh-heh! Now, is everyone ready?"

The wooden horses continued to look bored, as did the bellboys and a large percentage of the customers.

"Good-O! All right, Mr. Briggs, a twirl if you please!"

Briggs obediently gave the small cage a twirl and a gasp came from the audience, their ennui dissipated. The small wire-enclosed box seemed to explode; the three dice scattered about the general area. The library steward stood with his mouth wide, paralyzed for a moment; in all four-thousand-plus games he had directed this had never happened before. For a moment he wondered if possibly it shouldn't be added as part of the normal routine—it had certainly served to wake up the audience—but then he realized it would quickly lose its glamour. He hurried forward.

"Oh, dear! This little screw holding the bottom to the sides of the cage seems to have loosened. Does anyone happen to have a pocketknife? Ah, Mr. Briggs! And open, too. Thank you very much. I'll have it fixed in a jiffy!" He took the proffered tool and tackled the cage; it was only the work of a moment to correct the problem. He closed the knife and turned about. "Mr. Briggs—Mr. Briggs?"

Briggs was scrambling to his feet. He had located one of the dice and Captain Manley-Norville was handing him a second. A helpful passenger handed him the third. Briggs turned the three over to the library steward, who beamed at him.

"Ah! Thank you, Mr. Briggs. And your penknife."

"Thank *you*. No trouble at all."

"Ah, fine!" A small door in the cage was opened and the three dice deposited within. The library steward took a deep breath. "All right! Good-O! A slight delay because of unruly behavior at the gate, ladies and gentlemen, heh-heh! All set, Mr. Briggs? Then let them be off! A twirl, if you please!"

Briggs twirled.

There was a moment's silence; the audience waited expectantly.

"A pair of fours," the steward announced brightly. "And a six. Do you agree, Mr. Briggs?"

Briggs peered and then bobbed his tiny head. The bellboys dutifully moved their wooden charges the requisite number of squares along the green felt track. The steward smiled invitingly at Briggs, tilting his head. Briggs twirled.

"An ace," said the steward, "and another pair of fours. Do you agree, Mr. Briggs? Good-O, then. A twirl, if you please?"

Briggs twirled.

"Well, well, *well!*" said the steward. "Three fours! Imagine that! Do you agree, Mr. Briggs?"

"You had me sweating a bit until you clumsily dumped them and switched them back," Simpson said in a whisper. "I should hate to have seen number four winning for the rest of the voyage. Tell me, Tim, how on earth did you ever do it?"

"I never got arthritis like Billy-boy," Briggs replied, his voice low. "How much was the haul?"

"Thirty-four quid." Simpson sighed. "Unfortunately Captain Manley-Norville was back of me and he also picked number four. A pity I couldn't tout him off it, but there you are."

The two had risen and were moving toward the door, out of earshot of the racing fans who were crowded about the dance floor in expectation of the start of the second race.

"I think that's enough horse racing for tonight. Never push your luck, I always say." Simpson looked at his smaller companion expectantly. "There's a shuffleboard contest tomorrow. Do you have any ideas?"

Briggs paused, frowning, considering the problem, and then looked up with a nod.

"It strikes me," he said quietly, thoughtfully, "that a touch of powdered wax applied judiciously dead center just before the diamond should cause our opponents no end of trouble. Of course, we'd have to be careful and shoot for the edges."

"Beautiful," Simpson murmured appreciatively, and then paused. "But are there any prizes?"

"A pewter cup, I believe," Briggs informed him, "but we should be able to shame our opponents into a small wager, it seems to me. If we put our minds to it."

"I should imagine so," Simpson agreed with a smile.

He put his hand on the latch bar of the door and then paused. Behind him the library steward had begun to speak and he was not speaking of horse racing. There was also something in his

tone of voice that made both Simpson and Briggs swing about.
Their faces collectively blanched. Standing at the steward's side
and staring at them with no expression at all on his round,
pink face, was Billy-boy Carruthers!

"Ladies and gentlemen!" The library steward's voice rose
over the normal racecourse clamor. "One moment, if you please!
Please! If I could have your attention for a moment, please! I
have an important announcement to make!"

Slowly the din subsided. Heads turned to stare slightly re-
sentfully at this interruption in the normal process of losing
money. The library steward, in no way intimidated, beamed;
this time his beam looked quite genuine.

"Ladies and gentlemen! As I am sure you are aware, we are
privileged to have three celebrities aboard; the three winners of
this year's famous J.G.L.H.N.M.S. award. One of these gentlemen, Mr. Simpson, was a large winner in the last race. Now, Mr.
Carruthers, speaking for all three of the gentlemen, wishes to
announce that the winnings will be donated to the Seaman's
Fund!"

There was a moment's startled silence, and then, "Hip-hip!"
screamed a bediamonded dowager, and was promptly rewarded.

"Hurrah!" yelled the crowd.

"Hip-hip!"

"Hurrah!"

"Hip-hip!" It was the library steward leading the charge now.

"Hurrah!" The very rafters—the few ships carry—rang.

"That's torn it for fair," Briggs said with a disgusted shake of
his head and pushed from the room.

And Captain Manley-Norville, who only entered the games in
a symbolic fashion as part of his duties as host, paused as he was
about to place his fifteen-shillings winnings into his wallet and
frowned thoughtfully at the money in his hand. . . .

"I thought I had made it amply clear to you two reprobates,"

Carruthers said coldly, "that fiddling of any nature is out." He raised a hand to cut off dissent. "And please do not try to tell me that you won the game honestly, because you would be addressing yourselves to an unsympathetic audience. Nine straight rolls with three dice with a minimum of four pips popping up twice per roll. Really!"

"We were lucky," Briggs muttered.

"You were, indeed." Carruthers nodded his complete agreement. "Had you attempted that trick at one of the gambling clubs in Soho, most assuredly you'd be at the bottom of the Thames right now."

Simpson attempted to get a word in. "But—"

"There shall be no 'buts.' " Billy-boy's voice was adamant. "I told you before of this fine American author who was unable to sell a story of our adventures to this book club because we had not been as—well, moral, let us say—as we might have been. Should the opportunity rise for the poor fellow again, I should not like to see it lost because of your ill behavior. Is that clear?"

"Blast the blagged, bliggidy, blaggedy, blammery, bloggeldy, biggeldy, blattery American author!" Briggs cried with bitterness.

"I also understand this particular book club frowns on language," Carruthers said sternly. "So you might want to take that fact into account as well. . . ."

3

Clifford Simpson, stretched out in a deck chair for his afternoon snooze and looking somewhat like a tweed-covered pipe cleaner with closed eyes that snored, was suddenly awakened by having someone fall over him. He opened his eyes to discover an attractive young woman sprawled across him somewhat in the fashion of Limehouse Lil, a creation of his dating some forty years back, who, in addition to being an arsonist, a triple murderess and a bad cook was also oversexed. Still, Simpson was fairly certain the reason for the present assault could be explained on more logical grounds, albeit he still enjoyed the exposure of a length of firm, well-fleshed thigh and the fruits of an excess of cleavage pressed cushioningly into his face. But he did not get to enjoy them for long, because the young lady scrambled instantly to her feet, straightening her dress.

"Sorry, Pops," she said, with an effort at contriteness that probably wouldn't have gotten far with anyone, even Simpson, had he not been still half asleep. She tugged at her decolletage and then peered down it, as if to make sure she hadn't lost anything during her tumble. "I guess I must have been thinking about something else."

"That's quite all right," Cliff Simpson said gallantly and sat a bit more erect. He felt he might as well; he was sure that after that experience, getting back to sleep would be a problem. He smiled his forgiveness, pleased that his new plates permitted him to do so without clacking, and started to his feet. The young lady insisted upon helping him. Had it been anyone else, Simpson might well have demurred, especially since—even sitting—his hand was slightly higher than hers; but he had to admit it was pleasant to have a warm, slightly moist hand pressed against his with what he could not escape feeling was affection. Between the efforts of the two he came erect, towering above her. The least he could do in face of this aid, he felt, was to offer the young lady some refreshment.

"I say," he said, smiling down at her upturned face, "would you care for a spot of tea? Or possibly something stronger?"

"I'd give my arm," she replied, her tone of voice clearly indicating that having either tea or something stronger with the tall, thin man would be the height of an ambition nursed since childhood, "but my husband and me have a date with a couple to play cards." She smiled at him. "Hey, you're English, aren't you?"

"Yes," said Simpson, amused. "And you are an American."

"I don't know how you guessed it, but you did." Her smile remained. "My name is Carpenter; Mrs. Max Carpenter, but you can call me—"

"Max?" Simpson could not resist, he chuckled as he gave in to the impulse.

Mrs. Carpenter looked at him curiously. "Mazie."

"A beautiful name," Simpson said dishonestly. "I'm Clifford Simpson."

"Pleased, I'm sure." Mazie Carpenter paused a moment. "Say," she said, tilting her head skyward to view his face, "you look like a card player. Do you play canasta?"

Simpson smiled. "I'm afraid not."

"How about hearts?"

"I don't play that either." Simpson's smile faded slightly in the manner of one who had never before realized the full depths of his ignorance.

"Pinochle?"

"No."

"Fan-tan?"

"Fan-tan?" He seemed to remember Tim Briggs having advised him to use fan-tan in his story about Limehouse Lil, a story dealing with dark doings in an opium warehouse on Thameside, but up until now he had always thought it was something someone smoked. "No, I'm afraid not."

"Poker?"

"Poker?"

"That's right. Stud, draw, spit-in-the-ocean, high-low, one-eyed jacks or even Worcester, where a four-card flush beats a pair?"

Simpson was deeply embarrassed. "I beg your pardon?"

But Mazie Carpenter was not the woman to give up. "How about bridge?"

Simpson beamed, pleased to be back in the world.

"Bridge? As a matter of fact, yes."

"Thank God!" Mrs. Carpenter muttered.

"I beg your pardon? As I was saying, my partner and I—his name is Carruthers and you may have seen him about the ship, we're traveling together, and he's a middle-sized chap from top to bottom, that is, addicted to mustard-colored suits, though one mustn't call them that, and he has white hair and he's rather—"

"Pudgy?"

"I was about to say—"

"Fat?"

"As you will," Simpson conceded, not to be deterred from his one chance to fall into the grace of this lovely creature. "As I was saying, I believe we play bridge rather well. At least that's

the consensus of our club. We're the champions. Of course," he
added, his face falling a bit, "there are only three other partner-
ships in the club—most members play billiards—and two of
them are just learning. Bridge, that is, not billiards. Still—" He
looked up and then stared, struck by the utter coincidence. His
next line was one he would have deleted from any book he had
ever written—or even read—but still it came unbidden to his
lips. "But, here he is now!"

It was, indeed, Billy-boy Carruthers. He wandered up, smiling
a bit vaguely at the pair, accepted the introduction to Mrs.
Mazie Carpenter with his normal old-world courtesy and patted
his forehead delicately with his handkerchief.

"Say, your friend tells me you guys are hot at bridge. He says
you're a partnership," Mrs. Carpenter said, smiling in intimate
fashion. "That's sort of odd, you know, because me and my husband also are."

"Oh, ah?" Carruthers politely refrained from mentioning that
some eighty million other people in the world also were. "We've
played," he admitted. His deprecating tone of voice was that of
an expert going out of his way to denigrate his true ability.

Mrs. Carpenter bit back a smile of triumph.

"In that case," she said, "any chance of a game after dinner?
My husband and me are just learning the game, but we would
sure appreciate a chance of playing with topnotchers. They say
it's the only way to learn, and we sure want to learn. How about
it?" As an extra attraction she added, "I hear the movie is lousy,
anyway. J. Arthur Rank, whoever he is. Something foreign."

Carruthers appeared truly sad at having to refuse.

"I'm afraid that after dinner I'm scarcely at my best. Getting
on, you know. Early to bed and early to rise, has some salubrious
effect on a man, if I recall my Franklin correctly." He suddenly brightened as a possible solution to their problem occurred to him. "However, what about tomorrow morning after
breakfast? 'Man is at his best, they say, With ham and eggs to

start his day.' " He frowned in recollection. "Armour, I believe; or possibly Swift."

"Ten o'clock tomorrow morning, then," Mrs. Carpenter said coyly. Her attitude was such that had she had a fan, she most certainly would have tapped him with it. "I hope you don't mind a small bet on the outcome. Max—that's my husband—believes you only play good if dough is on the line. That is, if somebody has something to win by—" She contemplated the grammatical snare into which she had fallen and escaped as best she could. "—by, well, winning."

Carruthers smiled at her with pleasure.

"Precisely my sentiments, my dear. Your husband is obviously a man of great perception. Fortunately, we happen to be in a position where money is unimportant—if we lose, that is." He smiled at her with a twinkle in his blue eyes. "On the contrary, we might just come out ahead, you know. We aren't really all that bad. Champions of our club. I feel I should warn you."

"Mr. Simpson told me how good you were. I'm sure you'll nail us. But it'll be worth it. And we might just get lucky you know." Mrs. Carpenter glanced at her wristwatch. "Jesus H. Chr— I mean, good grief, I've got to get on my bicycle!" She smiled brightly at the two and disappeared in the direction of the card room.

"A lovely girl," Simpson said softly, shaking his head at the memory of her lush body pressed against him so short a time before and regretting—for one of the very few times in his life —the unfortunate passage of the years.

"Yes, indeed," Carruthers said, admiringly. "Clever, too."

"You think so?" Simpson's brow furrowed. "I had a feeling she was, but I didn't think it showed all that much."

"Oh, yes. Both she and her husband are quite clever."

He failed to explain this rather enigmatic statement until the two men had rounded up Tim Briggs, managed to find the bar and seated themselves in their favorite corner and had then ordered and been served with their usual. Briggs, being brought up to date on events, slid back in his chair and bobbed his tiny head.

"Oh, yes," he said. "I know the couple you mean. I've been watching them, as a matter of fact."

"Watching them?" Simpson said, surprised. He could easily understand anyone keeping an eye on the girl, but why anyone would want to watch the husband was beyond him.

"Yes, indeed," Briggs said, and picked up his glass.

"What Tim means," Carruthers said softly, "is that I asked him to keep an eye on the two of them in the card room—without their being aware of it—since the other day. And since Tim's the smallest, it seemed most likely he could accomplish the mission with the least chance of failure." He noted the query on Simpson's face and answered it before it could be voiced. "I've been wondering when and just how they would manage to approach us; and feeling that you would make the most innocent-looking target of the three of us, I'm afraid we left you out of the secret."

"Secret?" Simpson was properly bewildered. He set aside both his cigar and his brandy, a sure sign of perturbation. "What secret? What on earth are you talking about?"

"Well," Briggs said, taking the ball and running with it, "the two are cardsharpers. Twisters. This fellow Carpenter is an absolute master of manipulation. In our best days we couldn't hold a candle to him. He can do things with cards that shouldn't be allowed. And his wife has forty-five signals to take care of any contingencies, such as someone else dealing." He shook his head, almost in admiration. "A real cute pair, believe me!"

"And," Carruthers said, moving into the breach smoothly, "as a threesome who have just picked up twenty thousand quid, a fact unfortunately widely publicized, it struck me as logical they should attempt to inveigle us into some game of chance." He smiled gently and picked up his glass; it had all the air of his having stated verbally Q.E.D.

Simpson stared at him, aghast.

"And you and I are going to play bridge with those two? They being expert manipulators, and you with arthritis and me who has trouble shuffling the deck without dropping half the cards on the floor?"

"We are, indeed," Billy-boy Carruthers said simply. "And for as high stakes as we can manage to edge them into." He considered the problem for several moments, sipping on champagne as if it whetted his brain—which it did. "I should say we might well get them up to sixpence a point. If we use our heads, of course. We'll have to work out the necessary dialogue beforehand, you understand."

Simpson was stunned. The Corona in his hand burned itself to ash while he stared at his companions in horror.

"Sixpence a point? Against professional cardsharpers? It's madness! Insanity! They'll wipe us out!" He suddenly seemed to realize he was talking nonsense, especially in view of the gentle smiles on the faces of his companions. He pulled on the cigar until it was once again back in business and smiled ruefully.

"I'm sorry," he said contritely. "I apologize. Obviously, Billy-boy, you have a scheme. I assume Briggs will be in the general neighborhood to—well, somehow manage signals to us?"

Billy-boy Carruthers was honestly shocked. "Signals! I'm ashamed of you, Cliff!"

"But, then how—"

"This evening you shall—to coin a phrase—know all." Carruthers glanced at his watch. "Incidentally, I suggest you take up on that nap that Mrs. Carpenter so fortuitously interrupted. And Tim and I shall do the same. To build up our strength, let us say."

Simpson did not argue. Briggs grinned across the table mischievously.

"I have only one question," he said, his eyes twinkling. "You keep voicing this deep concern for this—you'll pardon me—

idiotic American author who lost some book club sale because, in your words, we weren't as moral in the past as we might have been. And yet, now you intend to take these card cheats for their life's earnings, obviously by dishonest means. How do you square these two?"

Billy-boy Carruthers was not at all dismayed by the question.

"You do not understand," he said calmly. "The ploy of the Biter-Bit is quite acceptable, even for the most puritanical of publishers. Or, at least," he added somberly, reaching for his brandy, "I hope so, for the sake of our American colleague!"

"Insomnia," said Mr. Carruthers sadly. His heavy cheeks seemed to have assumed the dewlap quality of a weary beagle; his blue eyes suffered from lack of sufficient rest.

"A terrible thing," the library steward agreed sympathetically. He was still, however, a bit puzzled that the tragic matter should have been brought to his attention, especially at one in the morning just as he was in the process of locking up the card room for the night. It struck him that the ship's surgeon was a much more logical person to approach, and being a man to whom the thought was father to the word, he voiced the suggestion. Mr. Carruthers shook his head.

"Pills," he intoned sepulchrally, making all pharmaceuticals sound like poison. "We aren't allowed them, I'm afraid."

"But—" The library steward paused as he suddenly saw the light. He only refrained from smiting himself on the forehead because it always gave him a headache. "Of course! I'm a fool! You want a game of sorts to while away the time!"

"Precisely!" Billy-boy's smile was congratulatory; it seemed to wipe away the dewlaps instantly. "Cards, to be exact. We wouldn't have troubled you, but the ship's shop is closed at this hour—"

"Oh, they don't handle them in any event," said the library

steward and unlocked a drawer. He reached in, extracting a deck. "Here you are, Mr. Carruthers."

Billy-boy glanced into the drawer. "Most interesting, I must say! How many decks do you have?"

"Oh, don't worry, sir." The library steward chuckled. "You won't short us, Mr. Carruthers. Fifty decks of cards we carry, more or less, for the use of the passengers."

"Ah!" Mr. Carruthers said. It was plain to see he was pleased by this bit of information. "Excellent! That will allow us to pass the time playing Burmese solitaire!"

"Burmese solitaire?"

"An excellent game. It takes three people and fifty decks."

"*Fifty* decks?"

"Exactly fifty, although it can also be played with forty-nine or fifty-one. Or even fifty-two," Mr. Carruthers said, with the air of one wishing to be accurate.

"But, then, sir—"

"Worry not," said Mr. Carruthers expansively, dipping into the drawer. "You shall have your fifty—or fifty-one—decks back by eight in the morning, long before the card room opens for the day. And they shall be as good as new. Better," he added absently, filling his pockets.

"I don't believe I'm familiar with Burmese solitaire," the steward said with a frown, and then added, remembering, "Sir."

"Few people are. Which reminds me." Mr. Carruthers paused in his labors, sounding as if he were answering the implied question in the other's words. "One thing, steward. As you know, we are—were—are, writers by profession. It is our intention in the not-too-distant future to put into print the vast intricacies of Burmese solitaire and thus slake this universal thirst for knowledge of the game. Until that time, naturally, the greatest secrecy is demanded. It obviously would not do to try and sell a book explaining a game if everyone was already familiar with the game. Surely you can see that."

"Oh, I do, sir—I do!" said the steward fervently. "It wouldn't make any sense at all. I can see that. I shan't say a word."

"I knew I could count on you," said Mr. Carruthers approvingly and continued loading the pockets of his ecru suit.

The card room of the S.S. *Sunderland* had the advantage of being properly screened from the Main Salon of the ship by a bronze grillwork while still being within hailing distance of the bar stewards who serviced the general area, and for this reason the Messrs. Simpson and Carruthers were able to maintain contact with the source of supply from time to time and thus stave off polydipsia. Both Mr. Max and Mrs. Mazie Carpenter, watching the brandy and champagne disappear at an amazing rate, could only pleasantly assume that what Max's ability with the pasteboards failed to accomplish, the ministrations of Bacchus were sure to do. The Carpenters were therefore more than disappointed—if that is not too slight a word—when, in fact, the fruit of the vine seemed to make the two old men luckier than ever.

Mr. Carruthers arranged his cards, spread them for study and smiled in a genial manner first at one opponent and then at the other.

"Four hearts," he said, and closed his cards.

Mr. Carpenter stared at him. He had difficulty believing his ears.

"I open a spade and you jump to four hearts?" He gazed back into his own hand, as if to be sure he had the cards he knew he had dealt himself. They were, indeed, all present and accounted for. He shook his head and smiled. His smile was genuine for the first time that morning. "I'm afraid I must double that."

"Fear not," said Mr. Simpson. He hiccuped, apologized vaguely and then nodded. "Redouble," he added, almost as an afterthought.

The proper number of passes having been made, Mr. Car-

penter led a card. The swift manner in which Mr. Carruthers
then proceeded to haul in the tricks and the undoubtedly inspired finesses he made not only to make his contract but to
garner an overtrick left the Carpenters sweating more than
slightly. Unless the old so-and-so had x-ray eyes or was in league
with the devil, he was doing the impossible.

"I say," said Mr. Carruthers, looking up apologetically after
he had marked down the score. "I'm afraid we're being terribly
poor winners. Could we offer you something to drink?"

"I don't drink when I'm work—playing cards," Mr. Carpenter
said a bit abruptly, and turned in his seat, raising his voice.
"Steward! A fresh deck, please!" He turned back to the table,
the falseness of his apology a sad thing to behold. "Just like to
change my luck."

"Just as well," Mr. Carruthers agreed politely. "Cards were
getting a bit smudged at that."

Mr. Simpson considered the score pad owlishly.

"And your luck could stand changing at that." His big green-
ish eyes came up warm with sympathy. "Are you sure you want
to play for stakes this large? As I told Mrs. Carpenter when I
met her yesterday, we were—or rather, still are, I imagine—the
champions of our club . . ."

Mr. Carpenter gritted his teeth and came to a decision. As he
was the first to proclaim at all times, decisions made in the heat
of anger are for suckers, but he could not hold back the words.
They seemed to pop from his mouth by themselves.

"You're right, you know," he said. "The stakes are all wrong.
How about doubling them?"

Both Carruthers and Simpson looked startled. Carruthers finally spoke.

"We've never played for more than a penny a hundred before, and here we are at a shilling a point! A shilling, do you
realize? And you're speaking of two shillings a point?" He pondered. "I really don't know—"

"That luck of yours can't last forever," Mr. Carpenter said, trying to sound jovial and missing it by a mile. "Thought you English were whatchacall sporting. Ought to give us a chance to get a little of our own back."

"He's right, Billy-boy," Simpson said. He seemed to be having a bit of difficulty with his words. He sipped at his brandy, took a fair draft of champagne and patted his forehead. "I say," he said, turning to include Mrs. Carpenter in the conversation, "it's a bit warm in here, don't you think?"

"Yeah," she said, and clamped her jaw shut.

Mr. Carpenter accepted the new deck from the steward and paused.

"Well? How about it?"

Mr. Carruthers sighed. "If you insist."

"Swell!" Max Carpenter slit the deck open with an expertly trained thumbnail, riffled the cards with a speed that defied the imagination and set about fixing himself an unbeatable slam. The time for subtlety was long past, he felt; the effects of four large brandies and half a bottle of champagne in the digestive tracts of each of their two opponents—and not even ten-thirty in the morning, yet—was clearly visible. He felt he could probably deal the cards face up without encountering too much argument from the old men. He completed the arrangement to his satisfaction and placed the deck before Mr. Carruthers for a cut he knew he could easily obviate. Mr. Carruthers' arthritis, aided and abetted by his multiple brandies, inclined to make him slightly sloppy, but he finally managed the cut, though it took him several tries and he had to straighten the cards as he pushed them back. Mr. Carpenter winked across the table at his wife, expertly dealt the cards, picked up his hand with a slight flourish and almost fainted.

"Hey!" he said. "These aren't—" He forced the words down his throat, though they gagged him. Mr. Carruthers was watching him calmly. "I pass," Mr. Carpenter said falteringly.

"I say!" Simpson said, arranging his cards and beaming. "You do deal wizard! I'll have a crack at two spades, if I may!"

"Pass!" said Mrs. Carpenter, barely containing a hiss, her eyes two dark smudges promising her husband a time he'd never forget once the bridge session was over.

"Oh, I say!" Mr. Carruthers studied his hand carefully, moved one card from one spot to another and looked up. "Two spades, you said, partner? Did I understand it was two spades? Well, we can't really let it go at that, can we? What about six spades?"

And so the session went. . . .

A group of players had slowly given up their own games to come and gather about the table as the play continued and word of the size of the stakes became known. Each miraculous defense play by the Mystery Authors Club champions, proving in each case the only possible means of defeating a hand, led the gallery to ecstatic "ohs" and "ahs"; each fantastic finesse or end play, every squeeze or coup seemingly anticipated from the very first card, brought admiring whispers from the growing group. Three more times Mr. Carpenter called for new decks; each one, if anything, seemed to bring him worse luck. Once he actually made the gaffe of staring at his talented hands as if wondering if they were betraying him, but a sharp kick on the shins from his partner made him quickly change the gesture into a minute inspection of his manicured fingernails.

In the crowd behind the four players, Sir Percival watched in profound admiration. There were several things his eagle eye noted and transmitted instantly to his giant brain: one, the Carpenters were professional card cheats and deuced good at it; and two, the old boys were making the cardsharps look like rank amateurs. Just how they were managing to do it, Sir Percival had no idea, but he was sure it was not through equal card manipulation nor through any extraordinary ability at the game of bridge. Whatever their gimmick was, he had to admit it was beyond his ken, and this irked him. Sir Percival was an avid bridge player who played for extremely high stakes, and while he was acknowledged to be one of the best in Britain, he still wouldn't have eschewed whatever trick the old men had up their sleeves. He was honest enough, however, to recognize he was probably the last person in the world to whom they would reveal their secret.

A deep voice sounded in his ear; he turned to find himself facing his old friend of many years and voyages, Captain Manley-Norville. The Captain was watching the play with narrowed eyes.

"Quite skillful, eh?"

Sir Percival smiled. "Which ones?"

Captain Manley-Norville smiled at his old friend briefly, but it was a smile that tilted his lips slightly while it did nothing to the bushy brows nor the steady gray eyes.

"Which ones would you say?"

Sir Percival laughed. "I'm the barrister, remember? I asked you first. Which ones would *you* say?"

"A good question; that's what I'd say," Captain Manley-Norville replied enigmatically and continued to watch the match with a thoughtful expression on his handsome face.

"Down three doubled and vulnerable," said Simpson, referring to the last hand played by the Carpenters, and marked down the score. His eyes came up. "My, my! This is somewhat of a rout, I'm afraid. Are you sure you want to continue at these stakes?"

"Shut up—I mean shuffle the cards and deal," said Max Carpenter between clenched teeth, and he stared fixedly at the cards as they slid across the table toward him, rather than look up and meet his wife's baleful glare. . . .

51

4

"So what's the story, butterfingers?" Mrs. Carpenter demanded. "Give me an alibi, and it better be good, Mr. Houdini the second—or maybe the fifty-second—because I'm in no mood for sob stories!"

Her voice was scathing; she was stalking their stateroom to the limited extent that shipboard staterooms, even luxurious ones, permit stalking. Her manner was that of a caged lioness deprived of her loved ones; which, of course, was precisely what had happened to her, her loved ones being Franklin, Jackson, Hamilton, Lincoln and Washington—or at least their portraits.

In the light of the utter calamitous disaster of that bridge game, Mr. Max Carpenter had become quite calm. The totality of the fiasco was too great for mere anger; it would have been like childishly losing one's temper at Armageddon.

"What happened, sweets," he said quietly, "is that we lost six grand. Our whole, entire stake. Plus, of course, what we picked up from the suckers so far this trip."

"Don't tell me bad news I already know! I know what happened! What I want to hear from you is, what happened?"

Bitterness tinged the normally quiet voice of Max Carpenter. "What happened is that we got taken to the cleaners by a couple of innocent-looking sharks who ought to be made to walk the yardarm, or be keel whipped, or something." Mr. Carpenter's ignorance regarding shipboard punishment was forgivable since he seldom saw much of a vessel beyond the card room. His tone indicated, however, that if discipline aboard vessels hadn't gone down a long way since Captain Bligh, Simpson and Carruthers would certainly have suffered the penalties described.

Mrs. Mazie Carpenter didn't even bother to sneer at this weak effort.

"Alibi Ike! Why don't you admit the truth—that you suddenly developed ten thumbs?"

"Hold it! Hold it right there!" Max Carpenter didn't mind being called stupid, idiotic, lame-brained, ugly, gruesome, dopey, and jerky by his wife—after all, marriage granted certain privileges that he recognized—but to have one's talent insulted, and falsely at that, was too much! "Don't tell me! I dealt those cards as good as I ever did! They jumped up and ate out of my hand!"

"Ate your hand, you mean—"

"Hold it!" He paused, thinking, and then struck himself on the forehead with his clenched fist. It was a bit harder than he intended, but as he rubbed the spot he didn't mind. "Do you suppose—?"

Mrs. Carpenter was far from sure this wasn't another ploy to escape her tongue. "Do I suppose what?"

He frowned into space and then brought one clenched fist down into the palm of the other hand. "Of course! Five will get you ten—"

"My husband, the gambler!"

"Hold it!" Max Carpenter reached for the telephone, dialed, and waited. At last it was answered at the other end; he dropped his voice silkily.

"Bell captain? I wonder if you could have a boy bring a deck of cards—playing cards, that is—to Stateroom B-67? What? That's right. From the library steward. Thank you. . . ." He hung up the receiver gently, remaining in a brown study.

"You haven't had enough cards for one day?" Mrs. Carpenter said sarcastically. She shook her head in disgust; it was not an unaccustomed gesture on her part where her spouse was concerned. "Or are you finally going to get around to a little practice? A bit late, of course, since we're flat broke. It would have been helpful if you thought of practicing a little last night!"

"Hold it!"

Mr. Carpenter raised his hand for silence; unaccountably, Mazie closed her mouth. Max seemed to know what he was about, a rare thing when he didn't have a deck of cards in his hands. They waited in silence; it was only minutes until a polite but persistent tapping came at the door. Max answered it, tipped the bellboy with a coin he knew he could ill afford at the moment and closed the door behind the uniformed figure, latching it securely. Mrs. Carpenter watched her small husband with narrowed but still suspicious eyes.

Max took the deck of cards to the small dressing table, switched on the light there and opened the deck with practiced fingers. The cards were first fanned out expertly and then regrouped. One card was taken and placed before the light; its opacity prevented even the slightest shadow developing. It was returned to its companions and the deck spread out on the Formica top of the table. Mr. Carpenter's thin index finger poked among them a bit, his small head bent over them, his sharp eyes studying every detail. For several moments silence prevailed; even Mrs. Carpenter was impressed by the thoroughness of the investigation. She stood behind her husband and held her tongue, no small sacrifice. Mr. Carpenter picked up one card after another, checking each carefully, holding them in his thin but muscled fingers. Finally he nodded slowly.

"Beautiful!" he said softly. Despite himself, admiration tinged his voice. "Lovely! Those dirty no-good bastards!"

"What?"

"Look here!"

He held up one of the playing cards for his helpmate's inspection. The back was decorated with a colored picture of the S.S. *Sunderland* sailing bravely into some exotic harbor. Mountains formed the background, birds wheeled in the sunlight over the smoking stack, coral sand beaches edged the blue water. Max raised his eyes to his wife's frowning face.

"What do you see?"

"A ship sailing into some sand, if it doesn't watch out. What am I supposed to see? Our six grand?"

Max nodded. "Believe it or not, Mazie, sweets—that's exactly what you are seeing. Our six grand. It's right there on the back of these cards, every cent of it."

It finally made it through Mazie Carpenter's irritation into her brain. The information shocked her.

"They're marked? Those old miserable so-and-sos slipped a marked deck into the game?"

"Not just one. A ton of them." Max Carpenter put that point aside for the nonce, sticking with more important essentials. He waited a moment from force of habit, allowing time for his wife to say something demeaning to him, but when silence prevailed he continued with his catechism. "See the smokestack? See the top deck? See the sides of the ship?"

"All right!" said Mrs. Carpenter irritably. Her previous silence had established a new record and she wasn't about to break it too quickly. "See Jane? See Dicky? See Spot?" She snorted. "I made it past the first grade. What's the pitch?"

Max Carpenter was not one to rush his triumphs. With his wife, Mazie, they were few and far enough between. He closed the deck and then fanned the cards widely, smiling at them.

"See the portholes? Those lovely four rows of portholes on the side of the ship starting under the Promenade Deck?" A thin, well-manicured finger came to rest, its nail pointing. "See? There's just the barest touch of shading in the different portholes. This card, for example: the first porthole from the front of the ship is a trifle darker than the others—the first porthole in the top row. My guess is either the ace or the deuce of spades." His fingernail flipped the card over expertly. "Ace of spades. So the card with the second porthole darker, would be a king. And in the second row, the king of hearts, and here we have—" He spread the cards with one finger and found his target. He flipped it over. "The king of hearts, as advertised." He grinned up at her. "Cute, isn't it?"

"Cute!" Mazie Carpenter was fuming. "Cute? Bullsauce! I'll have their scalps for napkins! Those crooks!" She reached for the telephone, sparks flying from her steely eyes.

Max Carpenter's hand closed on the telephone, depressing the button.

"What do you think you're doing?"

"I'm calling somebody, by God!"

"Who?"

"Who the hell do I know? Just somebody!"

"You're doing nothing of the sort," Mr. Carpenter said with a quiet authority that was so rare that Mrs. Carpenter didn't argue, at least for the moment. "Stop and use that beautiful head. In order to work their little swindle, they needed to mark every deck of cards on board. I switched decks four times, and it was all about as useful as pockets on a shroud. I'd give a grand to know how they managed to get their hands on all the decks."

"A grand you don't have," Mazie Carpenter pointed out.

"A grand, like you say, neither one of us has. Anyway, the fact is the old bastards managed to do it. Did you ever stop and think of that?"

"Are you kidding? Since you told me, I haven't been thinking of anything else! I couldn't care if they crawled over the side of this tub and marked the actual portholes themselves!" Her hand went out for the telephone once again. "Those miserable crooks cheated us out of six thousand big bucks, and I'm going to—"

"Mazie!" Mr. Carpenter's unaccustomedly sharp voice gave his wife pause. She slowly set the phone back in its cradle. Max Carpenter shook his head in disgust. "Use your head! We've figured out the markings. The cards are still in play; there aren't any others on this bucket! Take that fact, add to it you're crazy if you think I've lost my touch with a deck, and what d'you have? Christmas in July! We ought to send the old bastards flowers on their birthdays! They've put every other card player on this ship right into our hands!"

Mrs. Carpenter closed her mouth. It had been opened preparatory to scotching any argument whatsoever her husband might try to present, but the obvious truth of his statement took the wind from her sails. She considered it for several moments and then nodded slowly and, for the first time, with a smile. True, it was the kind of smile Genghis Khan most likely smiled when he first saw the banks of the Indus, but it was a smile.

"Yeah!" she said softly.

"And after the way we got slaughtered today, every card player on this tub has got to be convinced we shouldn't be allowed to play casino for more than a nickel a corner, right?"

"Yeah!"

"So getting suckers shouldn't be any great sweat, right?"

"Yeah!"

"And another thing: after the shellacking we took today, no-body in their right mind will ever accuse us of being cardsharps, which you have to admit hasn't always been the case. Right?"

"Yeah!"

"So," Mr. Max Carpenter said in obvious conclusion, "we should really be happy over what happened this morning. Right?"

"Yeah!" There was a pause. "Only I'm not," Mrs. Carpenter added, her voice harsh once again. "To be taken by a couple of old cockers, and foreigners at that! I'm telling you, Max, it doesn't pay to leave the good old U.S.A." She shook her head at the unfairness of it all. "Our whole stake out the window! Even if we know those cards like the back of our hand, so what? We can't play. Anyway, not until we round up some scratch."

It was the sad truth. The worst possible thing would be to jeopardize a beautiful scheme by being unable to pay for any temporary setback; and while they could not honestly foresee any setbacks, temporary or otherwise, neither one of them even faintly considered starting to take advantage of their knowledge without some folding money in their pockets. They had not foreseen losing to Simpson and Carruthers, either, and neither required a memory course by Harry Lorayne to recall that morning's session.

There was a pause while they both thought. Then, "Cable your grandfather? Collect, of course?" It was a silly suggestion and Max Carpenter knew it even as he made it. Mazie Carpenter didn't even bother to answer. Max wrinkled his small brow in further thought. "Do we have any friends with money?"

"We don't even have any friends without money," Mrs. Carpenter said. She didn't seem to mind the loss. She was thinking furiously, her pretty face screwed up in a frown. "The only people we know in this whole wide world with any loot are those three old you-know-whats." She paused, struck by a thought engendered by her idle statement, and then nodded slowly. Max Carpenter, no stranger to the weird moods of his wife, instantly became apprehensive.

"Sweets, what's on your mind?"

"The answer, that's what's on my mind!" She smiled, a humorless grimace. "Those bright boys are going to contribute a good chunk of our dough back where it came from!"

"And just how do you make them stand still for that?" Max

could not keep the sarcasm from appearing. "Just by asking them for it politely?"

"I don't know about the polite part, but you got the general idea. Yeah. We just ask for it," said Mrs. Carpenter decisively, and she proceeded to outline her plan to her husband.

Max's face blanched as he listened.

"Oh, no!" he whispered.

"Yes!"

"Not again! You promised me—"

"Keep quiet!" she commanded. "You just go get ready. And leave the rest to me. . . ."

Mr. Carruthers sat with his friends Mr. Simpson and Mr. Briggs at their usual corner table in the bar. They sipped their usual drinks in preparation for lunch as he studied the figure of the young bellboy wending his way through the laden tables in their direction and glanced at his massive pocket watch.

"A bit longer than I had anticipated," he remarked thoughtfully.

"I beg your pardon?" Simpson paused in the act of lighting a Corona and considered the man in the ecru suit curiously.

"The royal summons," Carruthers explained genially and turned to face the waiting bellboy. "Yes, son?"

"A message for you, sir." The bellboy produced a salver holding a letter. It seemed to come from nowhere—or perhaps from behind his back. Carruthers exchanged a coin for the missive and waited until the boy had left before tearing it open. He read it slowly and nodded, not at all surprised by the contents, although the stationery itself seemed to impress him. It was far more tasteful than he would have suspected and confirmed his belief that the skill of the Carpenters was seldom as unproductive as it had been that morning. He held it up.

"Rather nice, what? Monogrammed and embossed."

"What's it say?" Briggs demanded, always pragmatic.

"Oh, ah! Yes, of course. Well, as anticipated, it wonders if I might stop in and see her in her stateroom. Mrs. Carpenter, that is. It's cabin B-67." He smiled brightly at his friends.

"What's she want to see you for?" Briggs asked suspiciously.

"I doubt if it is merely because of my animal magnetism," Carruthers said. "My personal guess is that Mr. Carpenter— Max to his exceedingly few friends—has managed to discover the means of our success at the bridge table."

Simpson frowned through a cloud of smoke.

"I say!" he said. "They can't make us return any of it, can they?"

"I'm sure it would be difficult in their position. Besides, I imagine publicity is the last thing they desire. It would be against their best interests." Billy-boy shook his head. "No; I judge they have some other scheme in mind. Knowing the cards to be marked, and having solved the mystery of the markings . . ." He paused, thinking, and then looked up. "You know, that would make a rather good title, were we still writing. *The Mystery of the Markings. . . .*" He thought a moment more. "We might have this family named John and Mary Markings, and one day they disappear in a place from which nobody in their family has ever disappeared before, like the top box of a ferris wheel—"

"I believe that's been done," Simpson said thoughtfully. "Still, it's a lovely title. My suggestion would be a ringer in a pet show, winning because his trainer falsified his true markings—"

Briggs had had enough. "Dammit! Cliff! Billy-boy!"

"Oh, ah! Sorry. Got carried away," Carruthers said contritely and got back on the track. "Where was I? Oh, yes. The Carpenters, knowing the backs of the cards now as well as the fronts, and Max—being very fine in the handling of a deck— they are now in a beautiful position to take every card player aboard this ship. And we, of course—" He shrugged. "Well, we'd scarcely be in a position to unmask them."

"So what do they want from us?" Briggs demanded.

"Money," Mr. Carruthers said simply. "I'm afraid we depleted their operating funds." He finished his brandy, washed it down with a sip of champagne and came to his feet.

"But surely you aren't going to finance them with our money?" Simpson asked, peering up anxiously at the round face and innocent blue eyes of his friend.

"Not without a struggle," Mr. Carruthers assured him, and marched from the room.

In his youth, admittedly many years before, Billy-boy Carruthers had earned a reputation of something of a ladies' man, the reputation being relatively well deserved. The feminine form, therefore, was not a complete mystery to him. And, of course, on occasion one of the younger—or even older but livelier—members of the Mystery Authors Club would leave a dog-eared copy of *Playboy* in the club reading room, and in this manner Billy-boy had been able to verify the basic lack of design changes over the years. Still, there were figures and shapes, and shapes and figures, and it did not take a Praxiteles to know that the one standing and beckoning from the half-open door of Stateroom B-67 was one of the better models.

From her dress—or rather, lack of it—it was instantly apparent that Mrs. Carpenter might well contract pneumonia if left standing in the slight breeze from the drafty corridor, and for this reason Mr. Carruthers did not hesitate to enter and close the door behind him. Mazie Carpenter was wrapped in a diaphanous bit of transparent gauze that seemed to magnify her charms rather than disguise or hide them; her air of nervousness was not entirely put on, because it was some years since she and Max had been forced to use this particular approach, and she wasn't quite sure how well she was up on her lines.

"Mr. Carruthers," she said in a hoarse whisper, glancing about as if to make sure they were not being observed by any stray people who might just be wandering through the cabin, "you must help me! I beg you! You are the only one who can!"

"Oh, ah?"

"Yes!" Her hand grasped his arm, drawing it close in a gesture of confidence, inadvertently jamming it against her ample bosom. "My husband is an animal—a beast! And he is furious! He blames me for our losses this morning! Look!"

She drew back the sheer covering that protected her from the elements, exposing a bruised thigh. The large black-and-blue mark smelled suspiciously of lip rouge and mascara; the mascara had already begun to run. One split second was given for inspection and then the mark was instantly and modestly covered again. "And this!" A rosy tip-tilted breast appeared as if by magic, flaunting itself before his eyes, and was as quickly withdrawn from circulation, although not before a blotch of suntan powder had been exposed, simulating a trauma.

"Oh, I say!" said Mr. Carruthers, intrigued by the terrain if not by the seriousness of the wounds. "He did that, Mrs. Carpenter?"

"Call me Mazie."

"He did that, Mazie?"

"I just got through saying so, didn't I? I mean, he sure did! Max may be a little guy but he's terrible when he's in a temper. Hell hath no fury like—" She frowned; the words didn't seem right. She gave it up. "I mean, like Max when he gets mad! He goes ape, I'm telling you. And I don't know where to turn for protection! Only to you!"

She wound her arms about her own body, grasping herself tightly as if to keep inviolate its purity from the bestial grasp of her horrible husband and inadvertently dragging Mr. Carruthers' trapped hand into closer contact with her lusty charms.

"Have you tried the Captain?" Mr. Carruthers asked politely, doing his best to keep his hand from exploring.

"The Captain! That jerk!" Mrs. Carpenter snorted and then

remembered her lines. "I mean, poor Captain what's-his-name is so wrapped up in his duties, protecting us from the terrors of the sea, that he has neither eyes nor ears for poor innocents such as I, whose pitiful pleas must perforce fall upon barren soil and waste to nothing. What would he know of a woman's suffering at the hands of a sadistic monster? Only a man of the world such as yourself could possibly appreciate the tragedy of a mismatched marriage, the torture of being tied to a brute who enjoys—yes, enjoys—the . . . the . . . "

"Yes?"

"I got it! Where was I? Oh, yes. Who enjoys the beating of a soft womanly body, the silent screams of her misery under the oppressive degradation of his inhuman brutality." Mrs. Mazie Carpenter paused a moment to consider her words and then nodded, satisfied. "Yes, that's it. Inhuman brutality."

For one frightening instant Billy-boy Carruthers had the icy-cold feeling that the garbage to which he had just been subjected might have come from his own pen in those early days when he had been under the influence of J. Hamilton Grumbach. Then, with relief, he finally recognized the lines as coming from J. Hamilton Grumbach himself. They were from *Tillie, The Lighthouse-Keeper's Daughter;* and where Mrs. Carpenter had ever managed to unearth a copy was something Mr. Carruthers would dearly have loved knowing. His hobby was collecting dime-novel originals, and Tillie and her sufferings with the big lamp—not to mention the sadistic assistant lighthouse keeper who took over when her father was ashore for supplies—had been out of print some sixty years.

He fully intended to ask her, but at that moment the doorway from the bathroom sprang open with a jarring thud, and in the opening there appeared—as J. Hamilton Grumbach undoubtedly would have put it—none other than Mr. Max Carpenter in person!

Mr. Carpenter seemed to be growling or muttering, and he

had a frightful grimace upon his face. Whether he was unhappy
at finding his wife in their bedroom in a state of near nudity
with a stranger, or whether his unhappiness stemmed from more
cogent springs, was, at the moment, relatively unimportant.
What was quite evident was that the man was unhappy.

"*Eeeeeeeee!*" Mrs. Carpenter screamed. It was a well-con-
trolled scream, one that was calculated not to penetrate the
walls of the stateroom. Apparently Mrs. Carpenter believed in
keeping family problems within the family, other, of course,
than from saviors such as Mr. Carruthers. She thrust herself behind the rotund, elderly man, pressing her softness against his,
as if for protection. "Save me! Oh, save me! He intends me
harm! He intends to kill me!"

Mr. Carruthers frowned over his shoulder. "Are you sure?"

"I just got through saying so, didn't I?" Mrs. Carpenter asked
peevishly. "Open your ears, stup—I mean, you don't know him.
He's a beast, a devil!" Somehow, as if by magic, a pistol appeared in her hand, complete with silencer, undoubtedly taken
from the dresser behind her. She thrust it into Mr. Carruthers'
hand and screamed in his ear, making him wince. "Save me!
Don't let him touch me!"

It was true that Mr. Carpenter was advancing in small shuffling steps with a look on his face that boded ill for somebody.
Despite his smallish stature there was something about the look
on the man's face at the moment that was truly terrifying. Mrs.
Carpenter pushed Carruthers forward and screamed at him
once again.

"Use the gun! Don't let him touch me! Use the gun!"

"The gun?"

"Yes, dammit! The gun! Oh, for Pete's sake! Shoot him!"

"Well, all right, if you think it absolutely necessary," said Mr.
Carruthers, and, raising the weapon, he pulled the trigger. . . .

5

Sir Isaac Newton one day, apparently having nothing better to do at the moment, delivered himself of the edict that every action produces an equal and opposite reaction. The patent falseness of this ridiculous notion was never more clearly demonstrated than in the few moments following the discharge of the silenced pistol in Mr. Carruthers' hand; for while the gun merely made a little "pop" and barely bucked at all, the reaction from Mr. Max Carpenter was certainly far from equal.

At first his eyes widened in horror; he then grasped his stomach as if someone were trying to take it away from him. Following this he gasped, went backwards several staggering steps, pivoted to the right once and to the left twice, tripped over a footstool, tried to break his fall by sliding down the side of the bed, did a series of knee jerks, rolled over a few times until his head was resting on the cool tile of the bathroom, and then began to bleed copiously from the corner of his mouth. A few sharp twists and a final spasm and he lay still at long last, the blood running in a slowly coagulating wavering line to a small floor drain placed in the middle of the bathroom by the ship's constructors, possibly for this very purpose.

There were several seconds of taut, dramatic silence. Then Mrs. Carpenter slowly unwound herself from Mr. Carruthers and went forward hesitantly, peering down at her husband's remains. The sight was neither reassuring nor particularly appetizing. Her eyes came up, wide open, round with shock.

"You—you killed him!" She took the pistol from his hand and hurriedly hid it beneath the cushion of an easy chair, after which she returned to the bathroom and closed the door, hiding the hideous sight. She grasped Mr. Carruthers by the arm. "You must flee!"

"Flee?"

"Beat it! Scram! Damn it, don't you speak English?"

Mr. Carruthers frowned at her.

"But, I can't leave you alone with a dead body! What will you ever do with him?"

"Let me worry about that, huh? I'll manage, somehow. You just get moving! I'll be in touch with you later!"

She had grasped his arm in a grip of steel and was propelling him toward the cabin door. Mr. Carruthers set his heels and leaned backwards; in this attitude Billy-boy's fifteen stone made him a rather immovable object.

"Madam! Or Mazie, rather. Do you consider me such a cad that I would leave an innocent woman in a predicament such as this?" How now, J. Hamilton Grumbach? he thought with satisfaction and brought his attention back to the problems of the moment. "Quite obviously, we must rid ourselves of the body."

"You get out of here and let me handle this my way," said Mrs. Carpenter with evident irritation. She wished now she had enticed the tall, thin member of the bridge partnership into the cabin rather than this overweight ball of suet; not only did Mr.

66

Simpson appear to be less dense, but he couldn't have weighed more than one hundred forty pounds dripping wet, despite his immense height. At the very worst, she could have thrown him out of the stateroom by bodily force.

Mr. Carruthers eyed her with the indulgence one retains for women in shock and walked to the bathroom door, twisting the knob. He thought he heard a bump inside; when he had the door open the body seemed to have moved itself. Rigor mortis, undoubtedly, Mr. Carruthers said to himself, and studied the limp form. He looked up.

"I don't suppose you happen to have a steamer trunk?"

"A what?"

"A steamer trunk. No, I suppose not. They've gone out of style. A pity." He left the bathroom a moment for the stateroom, opening the closet and peering within. Outside of the fact that it was already filled with clothing, it might have done nicely, but obviously only for a short time. He frowned, considering longer-range possibilities. Mrs. Carpenter, feeling the affair was getting away from her, tried to bring it back to the original script.

"You—you killed him!"

Even under the trying circumstances that prevailed, Mr. Carruthers felt he could not permit this misuse of the English language; certainly not for the second time. Even J. Hamilton Grumbach, he was sure, would have objected.

"No, madam," he corrected. "I shot him. The bullet killed him."

He leaned over the body once again, studying the narrow shoulders, and then came erect, nodding.

"Of course! The porthole!"

He crossed the room to this most natural means of ridding staterooms of unwanted detritus, amazed at himself for not having thought of it before. He unscrewed the hinged bolts and pulled them away, tugging at the small window and swinging it wide. The bright sound and smell of the sea instantly filled the room.

"We may, of course, have to break his shoulders to get him through," he said in a slight aside and went back to the bathroom to gather up the body. A washcloth, properly dampened and applied, removed the excess of blood from the corpse's lips; thus having protected his ecru suit from being stained, Mr. Carruthers bent down and, with a strength surprising in one his age and build, easily lifted the limp figure of Mr. Carpenter, carrying it to the porthole.

During this entire scene Mrs. Carpenter had remained speechless, a rare situation for the lady, but at this point her paralyzed brain revived. She moved forward in a hurry, grabbing Mr. Carruthers by the arm just as he was raising Mr. Carpenter to the proper elevation for decanting.

"Hey!" she said.

"Yes?" Mr. Carruthers waited politely.

"He—he—well, he might not be dead, yet." It was weak and she knew it, but it was the best she could muster at the moment. J. Hamilton Grumbach, apparently, had left the matter of killing in a stateroom out of his works. In lighthouses he had no master, but shipboard cabins had never been his forte.

"It's really quite impossible to recover from a stomach wound of that nature, you know," Mr. Carruthers said in a quiet matter-of-fact tone of voice. He shifted the body to a more comfortable position, ignoring the grunt he thought he might have heard, and carried on. "Saw dozens just like him back in '16. Just suffered, poor chaps, but in the end . . . "

He managed a shrug despite the weight in his arms and turned back to the porthole, prepared to complete his offering to Neptune.

"But you can't toss him in if he's still alive," cried Mrs. Car-

penter, and added—rather inconsistently, Mr. Carruthers thought
—"That would be murder!"

"Much better to drown than go through the agony of a belly
wound," Mr. Carruthers assured her and started to feed the small
body through the round opening. "Drowning isn't all that bad,
they say. Of course, if there happen to be sharks . . . "

"Hey!" It was Mr. Max Carpenter, suddenly realizing the
discussion was getting out of hand and feeling the cold blast of
air on his face. He began to struggle.

"There, there," said Mr. Carruthers soothingly. "Just relax."
He smiled reassuringly at the pallid face staring at him incredulously from outside the porthole. He raised his voice to make
sure his words would not be snatched by the breeze. "You've
been shot in the stomach, and it's an excruciatingly painful way
to die. You'd do much better to let me get on with putting you
in the sea."

"You have to be crazy," Mr. Carpenter said in a whisper that
carried the first edges of panic. "You have to be mad! Mazie!
Don't stand there! Make this maniac pull me in!"

Mr. Carruthers shrugged and withdrew the body a bit, although he maintained a hold that would permit him to renew
his mission at any moment. Max Carpenter squirmed fiercely.

"Damn it! I haven't been shot in the stomach! Damn it! I
haven't been shot at all!"

"My, my! You mean I missed?"

"Max!" cried Mrs. Carpenter warningly.

"Oh, shut up," Max said crossly and squirmed more. "You!
Fat boy! Set me down!"

"Of course!" Mr. Carruthers instantly placed the dapper little
man back on his feet and bent over to examine any potential
damage. True enough, the checkered vest covering the small
torso remained inviolate, other than a tiny smudge navel high.
Mr. Carruthers shook his head in dismay. "I really did miss,

didn't I? And at that range, too! Dear me! I shall have to have my eyes examined as soon as I get back home." A sudden thought struck him and he paused, frowning at Mr. Carpenter with wonder. "But I'm sure I saw blood—unless I'm beginning to imagine things, as well. . . ."

"I fainted and bit my lip," Max Carpenter said with deep sarcasm. "Guns do that to me." He checked his appearance and brushed away a few spots that had occurred in his death-bed scene. His eyes came up to Mr. Carruthers' face. "Look, Buster—you've had your fun. Why don't you clear out, huh? Go back to your pals at the bar and get stewed, huh? On our dough, yet!"

Mrs. Carpenter was staring at the two men in profound puzzlement. Things were happening which were not in the script and she could not fathom why. She would have sworn that Bernhardt (had she ever heard of her) could not have turned in a better performance. Her eyes fastened on her husband.

"What do you mean, he's had his fun?"

"Just what I said. Old twinkle toes here was wise all the time," Max said in deep disgust. He picked a flake of dried chicken blood from the corner of his mouth, studied it distastefully for a moment and flicked it away. He twisted to see if he had sprained anything during his gymnastics, decided he hadn't and looked up broodingly. "He was having a big yak at our expense." He straightened his trouser creases. "We should have known better. This character is probably the guy who invented the dodge in the first place!"

"Not exactly," said Mr. Carruthers and settled himself in the easy chair, smiling at his hosts. The pistol with the silencer under the pillow disturbed him and he fished it free, tossing it aside. "Still, if you don't mind I should like to offer a bit of advice. The chicken bladder swindle may be fine on land—or, on the other hand, may not be, depending on many things—but aboard a ship it is fraught with danger. I mention this in purely

70

friendly fashion. One of the major points in the scheme depends upon the so-called corpse not being seen around and about after the event. On board ship it's rather hard to disappear, you know. And how would he get off the ship without going through Immigration? Or Customs?" He shook his head slowly and favored Max Carpenter with a pleasant smile. "You, my friend, are quite adept at handling a deck of cards. To be truthful, I envy you your skill. May I suggest you stay with cards? And leave these other dubious means of gaining a livelihood to those with the temperament for them?"

"Thanks a heap," Carpenter said in disgust. "Except you took us for our stake."

"Well," Carruthers said, coming to his feet and preparing to terminate a pleasant and enjoyable afternoon, "it's the rub of the green, you might say." He considered the phrase a moment and chuckled. "Yes. I must remember that. The rub of the green. . . ."

It had finally occurred to Mrs. Carpenter during all this conversation that not only had her memorizing and dramatics been in vain but that she had been made a fool of in the process. It was not a happy thought, especially for one of her explosive nature. She came to her feet and moved swiftly to the dresser, her wispy covering billowing in the breeze unnoticed. Pulling open a drawer, she fumbled in its interior a moment and came up with a small but efficient-looking nickel-plated revolver. Her hand held it steadily.

"Okay, wise guy," she said in a hard voice. "Fun's fun, and you've had yours. This cannon isn't loaded with blanks like the other one, and baby, you just better believe it!"

Mr. Carruthers did believe it. The look in her eye did as much to convince him as the small copper-headed pinpoints of light reflected from the chambers on either side of the stubby barrel. He sank back into the easy chair in a watchful manner.

"Mazie!" Mr. Max Carpenter had had about his fill of guns,

loaded or not, for a long time to come. "Put that thing away! What do you think you're doing?"

Mrs. Carpenter's jaw tightened ominously.

"I've had about all I'm going to take from old Humpty-Dumpty here," she said in a deadly tone. "Up to here! Either he lets go of a good chunk of our dough—at least fifty percent of what they rooked us out of—or I'll make him the saddest character who ever tangled with Mazie Carpenter, and that'll be a new record, believe me! Well, Fatso—which is it going to be?"

"Madam," said Mr. Carruthers with dignity—he did not feel that calling her Mazie would be appropriate at the moment—"I am, as you know, but one of three. For me to attempt such a portentous decision without consultation with my colleagues would scarcely be cricket. However, if you wish my hasty analysis of what the vote would be were the matter placed before a quorum of our triumvirate I'm afraid it would be strongly in the negative."

Mazie Carpenter turned to her husband suspiciously.

"What'd he say?" she demanded.

"He said no."

"Oh, he did, did he?" Mazie made up her mind. "Okay, Max, get on your bicycle. I'll handle this myself."

"Now, look, Mazie—"

Mrs. Carpenter swung about, a dangerous glint in her eye, "Now look what, Shorty? Are you going to give me a hard time, too? I said I'd handle it."

"No, no, sweets; it's only that—"

"Don't worry," she said demeaningly, in a tone that said she had read her husband's mind and as a result didn't credit him with any more brains than usual, "I'm not going to plug the fat little man. I'm only going to make him wish I had!"

Mr. Carpenter had seen his wife in these vengeful moods before; as a matter of fact, he had seldom seen her in any other. Mostly, though, they were directed against him and not utter strangers. He had never been able to figure out exactly what inspired the perpetual bitterness on which she seemed to thrive and had long since come to the conclusion that in infancy she had been weaned on vinegar. However, as a dutiful spouse he felt he should at least read her the standard warning.

"Mazie, you're making a mistake—" The look she gave him withered the words on the vine: he shrugged dispiritedly. "Okay," he said wearily. "I'll be up in the bar."

"Drink something cheap," she suggested curtly and waited until the door had closed behind her mate.

Mr. Carruthers continued to watch the lady with mild curiosity. As long as he had the assurance that he was not going to be —as the lady put it—plugged, he saw little to lose in enjoying whatever scheme she seemed to have in mind. Mr. Carruthers had a theory that women, given a decent chance to foul up a detail, will do so in direct proportion to the opportunities presented. Had he been called upon to give his hypothesis a name, he undoubtedly would have called it Carruthers' Law, with no attempt at false modesty. And he would have used both the ill-fated card game and the even more ill-fated chicken bladder swindle as solid evidence. What Billy-boy Carruthers had overlooked, however, was a postulate yet more ancient, which states that even a blind sow discovers an acorn now and then; and it was that acorn that Mrs. Mazie Carpenter now proceeded to unearth.

With an enigmatic smile from which Medusa might have picked up a tip or two, she walked to the telephone. Raising it, she listened until she heard the operator's voice on the line and then suddenly put back her head and screamed. Unlike her previous efforts which were purposely meant to keep the sound within the confines of the cabin, this scream seemed to be intent upon being heard as far away as the engine room. Mr. Carruthers, not having expected it, cringed from the onslaught upon his eardrums. The screech was repeated, even while Mrs.

73

Carpenter ripped the hairpins from her hair, destroying the work of hours, and rubbed one hand vigorously about her face, smearing her ample makeup.

"Rape! Rape!"

She suddenly seemed to remember the pistol she was holding. With the situation well in hand she recognized it was no longer required and could even prove a handicap, since few women armed with pistols are—statistically—raped. She dropped the receiver with a bang on the tabletop, walked to the dresser, deposited the weapon in a drawer and closed it, not lowering her voice as she did so. She seemed to be two people. One systematically disheveled herself in almost organized fashion while the other furnished vocal accompaniment in the form of banshee shrieks that raised the hair on Mr. Carruthers' head.

"My God, somebody save me! Take your hands off, you beast! Please! Don't! Don't!"

Never had the words of J. Hamilton Grumbach—or some imitator, were they not true Grumbach—seemed to Mr. Carruthers less comical. He had not bargained for an exhibition of this nature. To begin with, he considered it in the worst possible taste; and secondly the lady was giving him a severe headache with her racket. He came to his feet with as much dignity as the situation—and a low, overly soft easy chair—permitted, and moved to the door.

"Madam—"

Mrs. Carpenter was there before him. She reached behind him depressing the latch, effectively locking the door. Her faint smile indicated to him that she was actually enjoying herself.

"Cheat me, will you, baggy pants?" she said under her voice and instantly raised the volume. *"Take your hands off me, you animal! My God! What are you trying to do? Have you no shame?"*

"Madam—" Carruthers had to raise his voice to be heard; he knew his effort was wasted, but he still felt called upon to attempt it. "I'm afraid I must insist upon leaving. As for cheating you, that really isn't fair. You and your husband were fully prepared to cheat us—as you have cheated everyone else you've played with aboard. If you'll just calm down a bit—"

"Stop it—oh, stop it! Let me go! Don't—don't—"

Even as Mrs. Carpenter flooded the air with noise, she reached out and efficiently and effectively ripped Mr. Carruthers' braces free from his trousers. Since these had never been worn tightly— for Billy-boy Carruthers was a man who believed in freedom in all things—they instantly draped themselves about his ankles, revealing long gray underwear covering his shanks. Mr. Carruthers, shocked by this familiarity, reached down to pull them up; his posture allowed the lady to muss his hair and tug his necktie about, although these occupations did not at all seem to slow down the calliope sounds which continued to issue from her.

"Rape! Help! Beast! Let go!"

There was a loud pounding on the door and the sound of an authoritative voice.

"Open up in there!"

"Thank God!" murmured Mr. Carruthers and reached for the latch, one hand holding up his pants, but a whirlwind of pulchritude locked itself about him, carrying him backward. He back pedaled wildly, trying to keep his tangled trousers under control, eventually losing the battle and stumbling onto the bed. The continuing racket in his ear, he was certain, would surely result in permanent damage to the tympanum.

The sounds at the door increased as willing and manly shoulders thumped against it. There was sudden crunching of steel and the door flew open, swinging wildly, just as the floor steward came hurrying up with the proper key. In the doorway stood the ship's master-at-arms, accompanied by a husky sailor. Curious passengers peered into the room about the two official figures.

Mrs. Carpenter had slid to the floor at the side of the bed, whimpering into her hands, her hair scattered about her like seaweed, her sheer dressing gown torn and revealing. Trying to struggle erect on the bed, Mr. Carruthers was still attempting to untangle yards of ecru trouser legs that inhibited his ankles.

"Look at the old goat!" the master-at-arms said beneath his breath to the sailor at his side. "Didn't even take the time to take off 'is jacket!"

"Can't say as 'ow I blames 'im," said the sailor, sotto voce, and the two moved forward to take Mr. Carruthers into custody.

6

Captain Charles Everton Manley-Norville stared in frank astonishment at the short, portly, white-haired, angelic-looking man seated opposite him in his luxurious quarters adjacent to the bridge. Mr. Carruthers, quite comfortable, beamed back at him. The cohorts who had hustled him to this pleasant spot had been dismissed, albeit temporarily, and the two men were alone, basking—if that is the proper word—in the severe air-conditioning that kept the room a few degrees above freezing. Mr. Carruthers considered asking if his host's hospitality extended to a brandy, or something equally warming, but decided that this was not the place and certainly not the time.

"Now, Mr. Carruthers," said the Captain in his deep, rumbling voice—and it was evident from his exaggerated patience that he was repeating himself, and not for the first time—"do you mean to sit there and say that you aren't even going to deny that woman's charges?"

"And cast doubt upon a lady's word?" Mr. Carruthers made it sound like the most shocking proposal he had heard in a life admittedly spent among people who specialized in shocking proposals. He shook his head, his small blue eyes scandalized. "That wouldn't be very gentlemanly, now, would it?"

"Damn it, Mr. Carruthers! I'm serious!"

"So am I, Captain. So am I."

Captain Manley-Norville came to his feet and paced back and forth for several moments, coming at last to stand before his prisoner and glare down at him.

"Certainly, Mr. Carruthers, you are not yet so sen—so out of touch—I mean, certainly you must be aware of the seriousness of Mrs. Carpenter's charge?"

"Oh, I'm quite aware," Mr. Carruthers assured him. He frowned, thinking about it. His eyes came up at last. "Although I believe it isn't nearly as bad as when I was a young man. In those days, if I'm not mistaken, it was a hanging affair."

Captain Manley-Norville restrained with effort from saying that killing the king's deer was probably a hanging affair in the distant days when Mr. Carruthers was a young man. He stared at the seated man in cold silence awhile and then tried a different approach.

"I was a witness to your card game with the Carpenters, Mr. Carruthers, and frankly, I'm surprised. Gentlemen of your reputation winning a sum of that nature! I must say as well that I've heard it was nearly impossible to win from the Carpenters, and I was on the verge of doing something about it when you won that huge sum." The Captain reseated himself and drummed his thick fingers on the top of his desk while his steely gray eyes held Mr. Carruthers' innocent blue ones. "Well?"

"Well, what?" Mr. Carruthers asked politely.

"I simply mean that in the circumstances it appears to me that if anyone had a reason to attack anyone else, I would have expected them to attack you or Mr. Simpson, and not the other way around."

Mr. Carruthers was forced to acknowledge the logic of this statement, and his thoughtful nod did it for him. However, he apparently did not feel called upon to comment verbally. Captain Manley-Norville waited a few more moments and then continued.

"I don't quite know what your game is, Mr. Carruthers—and please don't be comical and say 'bridge'—but believe me, I intend to discover it. I don't care for mysteries on my ship. I've been master of the S.S. *Sunderland* since she was commissioned, and until you and your two friends came aboard, I've taken this ship on two hundred transatlantic crossings and over fifty cruise trips such as this without any untoward incident, and I don't intend to see that record smirched at this date—"

"I can appreciate your sentiments," Mr. Carruthers conceded politely.

Captain Manley-Norville disregarded the interruption. "—despite the fact that you seem intent upon doing so. Things are happening which I do not care to see happening on my ship. And you and your friends seem to be at the center of most of them. Well, Mr. Carruthers?"

Mr. Carruthers looked pained, as if truly unhappy that he could not find an answer that would satisfy the friendly and co-operative captain.

"Yes, Captain?"

Captain Manley-Norville drummed his fingers some more.

"Well," he said at last, "as long as you insist upon maintaining silence in face of Mrs. Carpenter's accusations against you, there is little I can do other than to keep you in confinement until we get to the bottom of the matter." He hesitated once again, as if waiting to see if this threat might produce some results, but when silence prevailed he sighed mightily and pressed a button on his desk.

"The fortunes of war," said Mr. Carruthers philosophically, and then looked concerned for the first time during the interview. "By the way," he said, "just how is the lady?"

"The surgeon is treating her for shock," said the Captain, his cold look of disdain clearly indicating his opinion of a man who could ask such a question in the circumstances.

"Better tell the surgeon to also feed her some good throat lozenges," Mr. Carruthers suggested in a kindly tone. "I'm sure the poor girl must need them badly."

The door opened, obviously in response to the Captain's pressed button, and the master-at-arms, accompanied by the same husky sailor, stood in the opening. The two maintained the wary air of someone called upon to pick up Jack-the-Ripper. Mr. Carruthers, properly assuming his interview was being terminated, came to his feet and then made a sudden lunge to keep his trousers from falling.

"I say, Captain—"

"Yes, Mr. Carruthers?"

"Would a needle and thread be permitted in the brig? The buttons for my braces are all gone in front, you see, and it's a bit embarrassing having my trousers constantly falling about my ankles." A sudden frightful thought came to the white-haired man. "I say, you wouldn't be taking away my braces, would you?" He assayed a smile that was pitiful. "I promise not to hang myself with them, or anything like that."

Captain Manley-Norville considered the rotund figure before him as if a new and not particularly unpleasant thought had come to him. He turned to the master-at-arms, speaking authoritatively.

"Give Mr. Carruthers needle and thread," he ordered. His eyes came up to consider Mr. Carruthers almost challengingly. "And under *no* circumstances deprive him of either his braces, his cravat, his shoelaces, or anything else of that general nature . . ."

"Rape!" Tim Briggs snorted. He was speaking through the bars of the small cell on E Deck where Mr. Carruthers was incarcerated. On one side a second cell of equal size and description existed, at the moment empty. On the other side of the cell the sound of the ship's laundry equipment working away at stained napkins and dirty towels could be faintly heard through a wall. The ship's screw seemed to be directly beneath their feet, throbbing rhythmically. Tim Briggs snorted again. "They have to be stark, raving mad! Loony as bus conductors! Rape! A man your age!"

"I'm younger than you are," Mr. Carruthers reminded him mildly. He was sitting on the small cot furnished by the management, straining backward a bit in order to sew on his brace buttons without removing his trousers. It made for a bit of contortionism.

"But not forty years younger, which is roughly what you'd have to be," Briggs retorted. It was an exaggeration, of course, but exaggerations had never frightened Briggs. He turned to the tall, thin man beside him. "What do you think, Cliff?"

Clifford Simpson was staring into the cell with his normal air of wonderment for all things in all places.

"I say! They really do have brigs aboard ships to this day!" he said, sounding properly amazed. "They actually do! I thought they went out with windjammers and leg irons!" He peered into the cell closely, as if to make sure—had they leg irons, or a cat-o'-nine-tails, or other torture devices—that Mr. Carruthers was not hiding them just to protect his friends from worry.

"Cliff!" Briggs was not interested in windjammers or leg irons. "We happen to be talking about this ridiculous charge against Billy-boy, here. Pay attention."

"Oh, I heard you. And I think forty years is putting it on a bit."

"Forget the forty years! What do you think of the chances of his really being held on such a silly charge?"

"Oh, that!" Simpson dismissed the "that" with a disdainful wave of a bony hand. "Silliest thing I've heard of in ages. Once this Captain what's-his-name gets a good look at Billy-boy, he'll have him out of here in seconds." He returned to his inspection of the cell. "I say, do you have rats?"

"No rats," said Mr. Carruthers. "And the Captain did get a good look at me. That's why I'm in here."

Briggs frowned in disbelief.

"And you mean he didn't believe your denial? The man has to be an absolute clod! Can you imagine allowing an idiot of that magnitude to run a ship this size?"

"Not even mice?" Simpson asked. He seemed to find it hard to believe.

"Not even mice. As for Captain Manley-Norville," Carruthers went on, "he isn't a bad chap at all." He finished with one button, checked to see that he had sufficient thread and immediately tackled another. "The thing is, you see, that I didn't bother to deny the lady's charges."

"You didn't *what*?" It was a chorus; even Cliff Simpson forgot his research on ships' brigs to join in.

"You heard me." Mr. Carruthers paused in his task to look up calmly. "I said, I didn't deny the lady's accusations."

Briggs stared through the bars in horror. He shook his head.

"You've gone crackers, too! Why in heaven's name didn't you deny them?"

Mr. Billy-boy Carruthers carefully completed the last button and snapped the thread. The needle was neatly tucked into the spool of cotton and put to one side. In common with most bachelors, especially those who reached his age, he was an excellent seamster, if such a word exists. He buttoned the braces in place, came to his feet and snapped them to make sure his work was of a relatively permanent nature. All remained secure. He smiled his satisfaction and only then did he bother to consider the question and to answer it.

"Tim, my lad. Cliff, old boy. Are you two seriously suggesting that I damage my self-esteem to that extent? Think what you are saying. Why, man, I haven't been so flattered in years! Accused of attacking a woman with immoral intent!" He shook his head, smiling, but the other two could see that Billy-boy Carruthers was deadly serious. "No, lads; I said not a word, nor do I intend to. I haven't the slightest intention of denying one word of the lady's story."

"He's gone around the bend," Cliff said sadly and then noticed something that had escaped him before. "I say, Billy-boy; I thought they took away your braces when they shoved you into quod. Standard operating procedure, don't you know, together with your shoelaces and things, so you wouldn't—well, you know." He made a gesture of a hangman's noose being brought up taut, followed by a neck snapping.

"You do that very well," Carruthers said approvingly and grinned. "I think that's exactly what the Captain had in mind when he allowed me to keep them." His blue eyes ranged upward. "I'm afraid, though, he never made a detailed study of this cell. I don't believe I could if I wanted to; the ceiling here is far too low." He shook his head forlornly. "They just don't build decks for hanging."

"Now, that wouldn't be a bad title," Simpson said thoughtfully. *They Don't Build Decks for Hanging.*"

"A great title," Carruthers agreed. "What does it mean?"

"Well," Simpson said, carried away, "you'd have this midget, you see, and he'd be put in this cell for something—cheating at Bingo, or selling tickets to the free cinema, or something—and this little man, Tim's size roughly, he'd be found strangled with his own cravat, and everyone would naturally assume the shame had caused him to hang himself, but then this chap from Scotland Yard—on vacation, of course—would turn up and study the scene, and he'd prove—"

"Yes?"

"That's as far as I see it at the moment," Simpson admitted, a bit unhappily.

"A midget roughly Tim's size, eh?" Briggs said in an unkindly tone. "Well, you'd have to lie down to hang yourself, Cliff, even on a scaffold. Now, if you two geniuses don't mind, I'd like to get back to Billy-the-Goat, here, and his problem. Whether you realize it or not, he's in the soup, especially with his attitude. Rape is a serious offense."

"Nonsense!" Simpson said, dismissing the idea as being idiotic. "Worse comes to worse, Billy-boy can insist on a jury trial, and what jury with a man on it over fifty would ever convict Billy-boy of rape?" He turned back to Carruthers, peering at him curiously through the bars. "How's the food? Crawling with vermin, I expect, what?"

"I haven't been here long enough to find out," Carruthers said dryly, "But I seriously doubt they'd go to all that trouble for just one customer. Anyway," he added, returning his attention to Briggs, "the charge isn't rape—it's 'attempted rape.' "

"Worse!" Briggs moaned. "Much worse!"

The other two stared at him.

"How so?" Simpson demanded.

"Well," Briggs said unhappily, "as you said yourself, no jury in the world would even consider rape as the faintest of possibilities where a man of Billy-boy's age is concerned. But *anyone* of *any* age could *attempt* it. . . ."

There were several moments of dead silence. Even Billy-boy Carruthers looked a bit thoughtful. It was, obviously, a point none of the three had previously considered.

"I'm afraid there's only one thing for it," said Clifford Simpson.

He and Tim Briggs were at their usual table in the corner of the Promenade Deck bar, sipping brandy. The third chair at the table was conspicuously empty; others in the room studiously avoided glancing in their direction. The master-at-arms, who also rounded up items for the ship's newspaper, had not been idle. Yet, despite the disaster of the previous afternoon, it was still a lovely day. Through the broad windows they could see people standing about the edge of the outside swimming pool while the lifeguard put them through a series of calisthenics, vainly attempting to remove in fifteeen minutes what his pupils spent eighteen hours per day putting on. The very sight of the sweating, jumping, miserable bathing-suited specimens outside made the bar both cooler and more cozy.

"And that is?" Briggs asked.

"That, I'm afraid, is something that will meet with your disapproval. Although," Simpson added, thinking about it, "we're really quite lucky, when you consider it."

"What will I disapprove of, and wherein are we lucky?" The brandy had made Tim Briggs a bit more mellow than usual.

"We're lucky that Sir Percival Pugh is aboard," Simpson said simply and instantly hid his face in his glass, avoiding the explosion he knew would result. He was not wrong.

"Pugh? That twister? That Jeremy Diddler?" Tim Briggs suddenly seemed to realize that his shriek of anguish had caused heads to turn. He dropped the volume but the tone of scathing denunciation remained. He hastily swallowed the balance of his drink and thrust his glass from him, as if thrusting Sir Percival away in the same motion. "Under no circumstances," he said in a cold voice, "do we get tangled up again with that—that—that legal larcenist!"

"Now, see here, Tim," Simpson said. Knowing Briggs, he was well aware that the first outbreak carried away the majority of the tantrum. "Try to be reasonable. Billy-boy is just stubborn enough to maintain his quixotic attitude, and this Carpenter woman is obviously vindictive enough to continue to press her charge. As things stand, therefore, the very best that Billy-boy can come out of this with is the worst of it. Now, you and I both know Pugh—"

"Do we ever!"

"As I was saying, we both know Pugh, and we know that he

85

could probably take the evidence in this case as it stands and end up having the Captain found guilty, even though he had eighteen witnesses that he was on the bridge at the time."

"Yes; and charge us an arm and a leg in the process!"

"We can afford his services. After all," Simpson said, "we did take almost three thousand pounds from the Carpenters, and even Pugh wouldn't ask more than that."

"Wouldn't he! He asked ten thousand quid to keep you from hanging!"

"Which I considered reasonable."

"Well, yes," Briggs conceded. "But that was a murder charge. This is only attempted rape."

"Look, Timothy." When Simpson used the full name, Briggs knew he was serious. "We can afford his services and we need them."

"Well, it isn't just the money, either," Briggs retorted. "It's—" He seemed to hear himself for the first time and was shocked to the core. "Well, of course it's the money! What am I saying? But I will admit I wouldn't mind it nearly so much if it were going to somebody else. Pugh! That twister!"

"Of course he's a twister; it's precisely why we need him. And there isn't anyone else. Certainly none to hold a candle to Pugh. He's the best there is. He's never lost a case."

"I know. . . ." Briggs gnawed on his lip for several moments in painful silence and then suddenly looked up, his expression of torment disappearing, to be replaced by a sunny smile. "I've got it!"

"You've got what?"

"The solution to our problem! The answer to Billy-boy's dilemma! We don't need Sir Land-pirate Pugh; he can go to the devil! We can handle this ourselves!"

"Oh, ah?"

Simpson studied the wizened excited little face across from his with cautious curiosity. Tim Briggs, Simpson knew, was far from stupid; in those distant halcyon days when they were all writing mystery novels Briggs' plots were usually far and away the most exotic. Imagination the little man had, and it was just possible that he might have stumbled onto a line of action that would, indeed, both free Billy-boy from the brig and also obviate the necessity of paying over huge sums to Sir Percival Pugh. On the other hand, of course, he could also be talking through his hat.

"What's the brainstorm?"

Briggs took several moments to savor his triumph. He poured himself a brandy and a glass of champagne, sipped at one and then the other, his tiny eyes glittering over the rim at Simpson. When he knew he had worked that ploy as far as it could go, he put aside his glass and leaned forward, hitching his chair closer to the table.

"Now, look, Cliff," he said quietly, watching his companion closely, "this idiotic charge against Billy-boy can only hope to stand up for a minute if this Mrs. Carpenter can be presented to the authorities as a mountain of virtue. Once this façade of rectitude is removed, the charge falls of its own weight. No popsy could hope for a second to get away with it. Right?"

Simpson merely stared at him with no expression, waiting for further amplification. Briggs obliged.

"Let me put it to you this way: if it can be shown that this Carpenter woman is in the habit of allowing other boyfriends to enjoy her favors—such as they are—her story gets pretty weak, and Billy-boy walks out of choky free as a bird. Right?"

"I suppose so," Simpson said slowly. "But do you have the slightest proof or even indication that Mrs. Carpenter is anything but what she appears to be—an excellent card cheat, a nasty-tempered young woman, as well as a devoted wife?"

"No," Briggs admitted freely. "Not at the moment. But it's early on, you know. Proof shouldn't be hard to come by."

Simpson frowned. "You think she's been playing around?"

"I haven't the faintest," Briggs said with a grin. "But she's going to begin to. Or, at least, it's going to look as if she had begun to play around!" He tried to look virtuous but only succeeded in looking more wicked than ever. "One has to fight fire with fire, you know."

"And just who is the fire she's going to play around with?"

"Me," Briggs said proudly. He seemed to recognize that honesty demanded cognizance of the possibility of failure. "If it doesn't work, of course, then I guess it'll have to be you. . . ."

7

In the novel *Soho Slaughter* (author: Timothy Briggs; publication date, May 1921) a miscreant alliteratively and euphemistically named Second-Story Sam, intending to rob the home of a well-to-do tycoon, quite properly took the sensible precaution of telephoning the residence first. Having cased the place thoroughly for several weeks, he knew it was the night the butler bowled and the cook visited her sister in Lambeth; but he also needed to know, quite properly, if the householders themselves were around.

The telephone rang the requisite number of times to satisfy Second-Story Sam that the abode was, indeed, deserted. He therefore proceeded the one block from the telephone kiosk to the house, his burglar tools concealed beneath his clothing, approached the place from the rear, or garden, side, shinnied up the rainspout, applied his jimmy professionally, and in a moment had nipped into the upstairs library where the safe was located.

His mind was on other things, such as anticipating the size and shape of the haul, and it was for this reason that he was halfway across the paneled room before he noted the presence there not only of the tycoon householder himself, but of his guest, none other than Chief Inspector "Fists" McFinch of the Burglary Division of Scotland Yard, and the scourge of all lifters in the area. Needless to say, Second-Story Sam was collared on the spot, and after he had been handcuffed and was being led to the door, he happened to glance at the telephone on the desk and to note the number. It was not the one he had dialed, and he was now paying both for failing to put on his bifocals when looking the number up in the directory and for not having rung the doorbell as a backup—or extra precautionary measure—in case of emergency.

Timothy Briggs well recalled the result of Second-Story Sam's oversights, and he had no intention of duplicating them. Before attempting entrance to Stateroom B-67, he fully planned upon not only telephoning but also ringing the small bell outside the door and following this up by knocking loudly on the panel. His problem at the moment, however, was not in determining the emptiness of the room before breaking in; it was managing to break in in the first place.

Second-Story Sam, while failing in the more essential things, at least had encountered no difficulty in jimmying open the window to the library, and if it had worked for Sam, Briggs could see no reason not, at least, to give it a try. It was logical to attempt it first upon their own stateroom, however, and to this end he brought Simpson into the action.

"You go down to the end of the corridor and cough or sneeze or drop something heavy if somebody comes about the corner," he said. "I'm going to see if any of the table utensils from breakfast might be used for getting open a locked door."

"Right-O," said Simpson amiably and ambled off down the corridor.

Fifteen minutes of profound effort, interrupted only once, proved completely useless. The spoon failed to give purchase, the fork bent, while the butter knife, apparently designed for other purposes, merely snapped. The doors on the S.S. *Sunderland* were fireproof and therefore of metal, and the products of Sheffield apparently were no match for those of Clydeside.

"Come on back, Cliff."

Simpson ambled back. "No go, eh?"

"Not a prayer." He thought a minute and then looked up. "Let me try a bit of celluloid slipped between the latch and the jamb. Got a playing card?"

"We gave them all back, remember? How about a wine list?"

Briggs considered it. "We can try. It might do."

The wine list did not do. In fact, it was quite evident as the two men straightened from the recalcitrant door that nothing less than a key, designed for that particular lock and no other lock, would or could do the trick. The two climbed the steps back to the Promenade Deck, wandered automatically to the bar at the aft end, dropped into their usual chairs, accepted their usual drinks, and fell into brown studies, seeking a solution to their problem.

The most logical spot to get a key, of course, was at the purser's desk, but the cubbyholes of this domain were well—and seemingly perpetually—guarded by a uniformed junior purser-type who apparently neither ate nor slept. There was, of course, the possibility that more than one man was in attendance at different times and that they all merely looked so much alike that one couldn't tell them apart, but this really contributed little to the solution to the problem. It appeared obvious that in order to gain access to the key rack, the junior attendant of the moment was going to have to be lured from his post. Briggs suddenly looked up.

"Cliff, could you reach the key rack from the front of the desk? I mean, without having to waste time going behind the counter? If I could get the purser-type's attention off to one side for a moment, say? Or manage to have him run some sort of errand?"

Simpson thought about it, trying to picture approximately where the cubbyhole for Stateroom B-67 was located. "I could try, I suppose."

"Can't ask more than that," Briggs said logically and came to his feet. The two men retraced their steps, leaving their drinks in a state that would assure the bar steward of their return.

The purser's square was empty, a not unusual condition for that time of the day—empty, that is, except for the attendant who smiled at them alertly from behind his counter. Simpson's eye located the tiny box assigned to Stateroom B-67 and noted with pleasure that a key did, indeed, rest therein. He leaned against the counter gently, calculating angles and distances. It was possible. The purser smiled at them again, but it promised to be the last smile unless some task was demanded of him soon.

"Yes, gentlemen?"

"I do believe I'm not feeling well at all," Briggs said, and did his best to look the part. The purser's eyes swiveled in his direction. "I say, I don't suppose you might dash about the corner to the dining room and get me a glass of water, could you?"

Simpson stared at his partner in crime with a startled expression. The thought of Briggs requesting water was incredible; but then he recalled that people supposedly feeling ill quite often drank water. It was difficult to comprehend, but there you were. His eyes moved from Briggs to the uniformed purser. This one was hesitating, painfully torn between his oath to Aid Passengers, and his duty Not to Leave His Post. He attempted to resolve both his problems at once.

"Possibly if I were to ring through to the surgeon's office, sir?"

"I don't want an operation," Briggs said curtly. "My heavens! A simple glass of water!"

"Oh, ah!" said the purser, recognizing the logic of the other's position.

He sighed and slipped from behind his counter, determined—if he had to get water—to get water at a speed no other junior purser-type would duplicate for years. He disappeared about a corner. Simpson winked at Briggs in congratulation and stretched, leaning as far forward as his extreme height permitted. By going tippy-toe, it appeared that he could just make it.

And then, "Suffering the cramp, Mr. Simpson?"

The deep, unexpected voice behind him very nearly made Mr. Simpson suffer heart seizure as well as cramp. He straightened up guiltily and turned; Briggs had also swung about. Captain Charles Everton Manley-Norville, never more magnificently uniformed nor more authoritative in stature, was eyeing them from the stairway with cold sardonicism.

"A touch," Simpson managed, at which moment the purser returned bearing water. Before the glass could be delivered to the proper patient, Simpson had grasped it eagerly and was drinking frantically. "Thanks ever so much," Simpson said, fighting down the taste of the water, and escaped up the steps with Briggs at his side. Captain Manley-Norville stared after them thoughtfully a moment, gave the junior purser-type a glare to remind him about Not Leaving His Post Under Any Circumstances, and marched off down a corridor, continuing with his daily inspection of his ship.

"A sneak!" Briggs said bitterly. "Rubber-soled shoes! Now, I ask you—what way is this to run a ship? Doesn't he ever go up on the bridge—just to visit, let's say?"

Simpson had no answer; besides, he was busily removing the taste of water from his mouth with brandy. Silence reigned again for several minutes. Then Briggs sat a bit more erect.

"I know!" he said, and came to his feet. He nodded at Simpson somberly and disappeared through the doorway leading to the deck. In exactly ten minutes he returned, looking downhearted, and took his seat again. Simpson merely raised an inquisitive eyebrow in his direction.

"Went and bought a shilling shocker," Briggs explained curtly. "Waited until the purser turned his back a minute and then took this paperback book out of my pocket and put it on the floor. Then I said to him, 'Chap just dropped this,' I said. 'If you hurry you can probably catch him. He just trotted up the steps.' "

Simpson was giving the tale his fullest attention. "And?"

"And this purser-type looks at me as if I'd been scaling fish all morning, and he says, 'Thank you,' and he opens a drawer and drops the book inside. 'Whoever lost it will be coming back here looking for it,' he says. 'This is the lost-and-found department, among other things.' And that was that. Actually cost two and six, not a shilling," he added almost absently.

"Hard lines," Simpson said sympathetically. "Well while you were gone I had a idea myself that might work. If you'll pardon me. . . ." He came to his feet, unfolding himself carefully as if to make sure he didn't break in the process.

"Be my guest," Briggs said gloomily and reached out for the bottle, pouring himself another drink.

Clifford Simpson, at least, was speedier than his shorter companion, although this may have been because of the greater length of his stride. In any event, he returned in eight minutes, looking no happier than had Briggs upon his return. Briggs recognized the symptoms; he poured a second glass of brandy for his old friend and silently pushed it across the table.

Simpson accepted it with a nod of appreciation, sipped it gratefully and began his own tale of woe.

"My plan was eminently simple," said he. "I realized that in requesting water, we were, in fact, asking the man to undertake a mission not truly within his scope of authority. Bellboys carry water; dining room stewards carry water—even, on occasion, bar stewards. Purser-types do not carry water. Do you follow me?" he asked anxiously.

"So far."

"Fine! However, were we to ask the man to perform a duty consistent with the purposes of the purser's department, he'd be rather hard put to avoid it, what?"

"So far still so good."

"Yes. I therefore calculated I would merely ask this purser-type to be so kind as to bring me a bit of our luggage from the hold—"

"We don't have any luggage in the hold."

"So he pointed out," Simpson said sadly. "It seems they have a small file in a drawer there with a list of everyone's luggage that is stored in the hold. So when he started looking through this file to find out which hold, and what section, and all the rest of it, he quickly discovered that, as you said, we had no luggage in the hold. So I could only stand there looking absent-minded, pretend my cramp had returned, and get out of there as quickly as possible."

"A bit embarrassing, I imagine."

"Yes." Simpson frowned, putting the incident from his mind like a good soldier, returning to business. "Do you suppose the call of 'Fire!' might get him to move away from that counter of his?"

"I doubt it," Briggs said sourly. "All those purser-types look the kind to go down with the desk."

Again there was silence, and then, "I say," Simpson said, sitting a bit more erect. "Maybe the Carpenters might just wander out of their stateroom and leave the door open. Forget to lock it, you know."

"Not exactly the epitome of expert planning on our part if they did," Briggs said dryly and shook his tiny head. "Anyway, they couldn't if they wanted to. Door locks automatically when it closes. You have to have a key to open it. They have a notice to that effect posted in the cabin. Haven't you seen it?"

"I don't recall," Simpson said sadly and leaned back again.

Silence returned once again; this time Briggs broke it.

"There's no sense sitting here doing nothing," he said and came to his feet. "I'm going down and look at the blasted cabin, even if I can't figure out how to get in. No," he added truthfully, seeing the question in his friend's eye, "I haven't the vaguest notion what earthly use it might be, but it has to be at least as useful as sitting here stewing." He raised a hand. "Ta."

"Ta," said Simpson, and watched him disappear.

The fresh air on deck and the bright sun in the sky did nothing to cheer Briggs as he made his way forward toward the entrance to the main companionway and started down the broad carpeted steps. For one thing his mind was not on his surroundings but was still tackling the delicate problem of how to get a key to Stateroom B-67.

Bribe the steward or the stewardess who tended that portion of B Deck? Far too dangerous; stewards and stewardesses lead solitary lives, relieved only by gossip in their few free moments. No, wipe out bribery; besides, it cost money, and Timothy Briggs only spent money as a last resort. He shook his head and passed A Deck, descending steadily, still studying the problem.

Possibly if he waited until he saw the Carpenters at the pool they might leave their room key in a swimming robe—except they never went swimming. Pick their pocket in the cinema? Again, since the films were all British and therefore foreign, the Carpenters remained loyal Americans and stayed away. What to do?

What would Second-Story Sam have done that fateful night in 1921 if the library window had been made of steel and required a key? Probably given it up as a bad job, Briggs thought, coming to B Deck and turning down a corridor. Either that or used dynamite. These chaps on TV always seem to have little gadgets they remove from their lapels to put into the lock and apply a match and the things just go *phzzz* and emit a trifle of smoke and *voilà!* the door swings open, all in dead silence and with no trouble at all. Unfortunately, in real life getting through a solid door was far from being that simple. What to do? What in the devil to do?

In his concentration on his problem, Briggs was unaware for several moments of the man who was addressing him. When at last he realized the extra voice he was hearing was not coming from his subconscious, he looked up, finally paying attention. Before him a mechanic-type in stained coveralls and wearing a greasy cap pushed far back on his head was apparently trying to communicate.

"—bustit it wide open they did, when they crashit in to grab that nasty 'ol chap," the man in the coveralls was saying.

"What?"

"Raht!" said the other, as if Briggs had made a valuable contribution to the conversation. "Raht offen the 'inges practically! O' course they was two o' them—that master-at-arms he couldn't bust a paper bag."

"I beg your pardon?"

"Well, he couldn't. Anyways," the man in the coveralls went on, "I just finished fixin' it and puttin' in a new lock. 'ad to put on new 'inges, too."

Briggs frowned at the man. "Would you mind telling me what you're talking about?"

"I was saying it's all fixed, like. But they don't like us shop people goin' up inter the purser's square dressed like this. An' the folks what got the cabin ain't in."

Briggs stared at him. "So?"

"I was only askin' as a favor, like, sir. If you was goin' near the purser's square and the counter there was orl I was askin'." He sounded put upon.

"What *are* you mumbling about?" Briggs demanded.

"I was just askin' if you could drop them off, was orl, sir." He dug into his pocket and came up with two sets of keys. "If you was near there, sir. They don't like us shop people up inter the purser's square dressed like this."

Briggs swallowed. "Happy to," he heard himself say, and heard himself add, "A pleasure." He watched his own hand reach out in a daze and accept the keys; it was somewhat like seeing one of those mechanical arms in an isotope laboratory extending as if by magic to pick up a crucible of something precious.

"Thank yer, sir," said the mechanic-type. He picked up his tool kit with one hand and touched the brim of his cap with the other. "Yer a real gent." And he pushed through a small door and disappeared.

"Well, well," said Briggs softly, and grinned.

The cabin was dim when he entered, with the drapes drawn over the porthole. He did not bother to set the inner latch, considering that since he was the sole possessor at the moment of keys to the lock, interruption was impossible. Had he thought of the master key in the hands of the stewardess he might not have been quite so insouciant, but he didn't and was fortunate enough not to have to during the course of his intrusion. But then Briggs undoubtedly would have felt that his luck having changed, it deserved to maintain a steady course for awhile, at least. With a grin at the thought of the look on Simpson's face when he heard how entrance was finally accomplished, he pulled the curtains free from the porthole and set to work.

Briggs' plan was extremely simple. To begin with, he recalled vividly the private stationery Mrs. Carpenter had used in writing Carruthers his invitation to the chicken-bladder swindle, and he intended to stock up on enough of it so that, at a later and more leisurely hour, he could dash off a few compromising notes addressed to various nonexistent males. He was certain he was still up to managing a reasonable facsimile of the woman's scrawling handwriting; and he was also sure his sense of inventiveness would make the things sound sufficiently damaging in court. Search for the stationery was practically unnecessary; it stood in plain sight atop the dresser, and he pocketed a sufficient quantity before moving to step two of the plan.

In truth, the writing of compromising letters might better be called Step Two of the plan, since they were, in actuality, a sort of back up to the main body of the scheme, to be used only if all else failed. The main essence of the plan was nothing as subtle as compromising letters; Briggs intended to be seen by reliable witnesses leaving Mrs. Carpenter's stateroom in a state of dishevelment normally attributed only to lovemaking. To this end, the stationery having been taken care of, he turned to the dressing table.

A series of bottles, jars, tubes and flasks of various shapes and colorations dotted the surface. He opened one of the more glamorous-looking bottles, smelled it and winced. Inspection of the ornate label identified it as a corn cure; he capped it and tried another. Here luck was with him, for while the aroma still made him cringe, it was only because of its excessive sweetness. He smiled and dabbed enough about his person to make him reek. The second step was to discover the lipstick, and this was made easier by the shape of the container. A little of the glossy orange-red color went a long way. He checked his appearance in the mirror, added a dab of lipstick to his shirt collar, pulled his tie about and winked at his image roguishly. The few seconds spent in the cabin had definitely been of value, and the trick now was to be seen leaving the room. He checked to make sure everything had been handled according to schedule, pulled the drapes back across the porthole, giving the room the proper dimness suitable for romance, and then moved to the door.

The advantages of steel doors aboard ships are many, of course; they have a tendency to outlast wood in service, they do not burn, and—as Briggs and Simpson could testify—they prove quite difficult for unauthorized personnel to enter. Their major disadvantage, however, is that they are exceedingly hard to listen through. Briggs, pressing his tiny ear tightly against the smooth panel and hoping to encounter footsteps passing in the corridor without, only felt the vibration of the ship's engines magnified tenfold through the cold metal. Nottingham could have been playing Newcastle rugger in the corridor and he would have missed it. With a shrug, he opened the door and peeked out.

The slightly tilted aisle was deserted. He was not worried about the Carpenters returning; it was his understanding that they undeviatingly followed a pattern of card playing when they were not eating or sleeping. Still, he did feel that traffic on B Deck, even without the Carpenters, could have been a bit heavier; that someone—a steward, a stewardess, a passenger, a waiter—anyone, in fact, other than Captain Manley-Norville—ought to be using the corridor for some purpose or other. He was on the verge of returning to the telephone and calling Simpson to send a bellboy down to B Deck on some excuse or other when his prayers were finally answered. Turning the corner and moving slowly in his direction was a figure that could be identified as a steward because of its white jacket, even at that great distance. It was all that Tim Briggs had been waiting for.

Without wasting further time he swung the door wide and stepped smartly out into the corridor, purposely refraining from glancing in the direction of the approaching steward. With a theatrical ability he had long suspected himself capable of, he made an exaggerated gesture of blowing a kiss toward an invisible occupant of the room.

"I'll see you around and about, lovey," he said in a loud tone of voice. He was sure his words were audible the length of the corridor, but even if they weren't, the smell of that awful perfume was sure to be. "Mind, now, don't stand in a draft like that without any clothes; you'll catch your death."

He reached out and closed the door with the air of the protector, after which he swaggered manfully off down the corridor, keeping his back to the white-jacketed figure, making it quite evident to all that he considered himself unseen.

Once about the corner, he nipped briskly up the steps to A Deck and hurried to their cabin. The door was closed behind him and latched; he leaned against it, breathing deeply. Unfortunately, the inhalation brought the full power of Mrs. Carpenter's perfume to his nostrils; it was enough to remind him to get cracking. The stationery was stowed in a drawer for future use, after which he scrubbed in a real steaming-hot shower and changed his clothing from skin out before he felt fit to leave the cabin. He had a feeling that Simpson would not be overly pleased with the cloying stench of the laundry he had tossed in the closet, but then, he said to himself as he closed the door behind him, one can scarcely make omelettes without breaking eggs. Although respectable eggs, of course, really shouldn't smell. . . .

He paused long enough to drop the keys to Stateroom B-67 in a corner where some curious passenger was bound to notice them and turn them into the purser's desk, after which he climbed the rest of the steps with an inward grin, made his way to the bar and fell into his chair opposite Simpson, looking like the Cheshire cat. Simpson looked up from his cerebrations, frowning.

"You know?" he said thoughtfully, "I think I've got it all figured out. If you could get over the side, somehow, you're small enough to crawl through the porthole . . . "

"Don't worry about it," Briggs said a trifle grandly, waving his hand. "It's all been handled."

"What's all been handled?"

"The hash of those Carpenter twisters—that's what's all been handled!" said Briggs, and laughed aloud. It was a joyous, strident laugh; he suddenly realized he was being a bit noisy and that other customers in the bar were staring at him strangely. He dropped his voice but retained his grin. "Wait until you hear!" he said, his tiny eyes twinkling merrily. "Just wait until you hear!"

Mrs. Penelope Watkins, age forty-three, had been a stewardess aboard the S.S. *Sunderland* as long as Captain Manley-Norville had been its master, and in the course of the many years she had learned to be shocked by few things. Naughtiness, she had long since found, seemed to be a concomitant of shipboard travel; she was sure that had marriage certificates been required of passengers in lieu of visas, cruise trips would completely disappear. However, the story told her by the steward that a tiny, wrinkled old man smelling to high heaven of scent and talking some nonsense about the woman inside putting on her clothes to avoid catching cold immediately sent Mrs. Watkins to investigate. As mentioned before, it wasn't that she was particularly worried about the morals involved; it was simply that she knew the Carpenters were never in their cabin at that hour and that therefore anyone seen coming from Stateroom B-67 could only be a sneak thief, although how the wrinkled little old man had gained entrance was a complete mystery to her. She knew the lock had been changed by a mechanic-type just a few moments before, and she knew she had one of the two master keys in that section.

She rang the small bell set in the door lintel, waited a proper time and then used the key itself to knock against the metal panel of the door. Experience had long since proven this to be a far more carrying—not to mention, irritating—sound. When there was no response, she felt her fears had been justified; she opened the door and peered within. Everything seemed to be in its proper place; she came further into the room and pulled aside the drapes concealing the porthole, examining the room in the greater light that poured in, reflected from the bright sea. The steward must have been drunk and imagining things, she thought, because not a thing had been touched. A few coins on the dresser were still there; even Mrs. Carpenter's wristwatch was in plain sight on the end table beside the bed, and while it wasn't diamond studded, what sneak thief would have overlooked it merely because it lacked brilliants? The steward, clearly, had been dreaming.

She pulled the drapes back in place and, from force of habit, smoothed the already wrinkle-free bedspread. The next task, also done from habit, was to check the bathroom for towel requirements. The light switch was on the outside; she flicked it on and pushed the door open, glancing at the towel rack. The full complement of drying equipment was present. The last possible lack was, of course, washcloths, and to investigate the status of these, she drew the shower curtain. And then she screamed and screamed and screamed and screamed and screamed.

Mrs. Carpenter—or rather, her nude body—was lying in a twisted position on the cold tile floor of the shower stall. She seemed to be wearing a bandeau of red about her ample bosom, but on closer inspection, Mrs. Watkins saw that it was merely the flow of blood from the many stab wounds in her chest. . . .

8

Sir Percival Pugh, relaxing with a book on legalistic maneuvers, was really not greatly astonished to find his solitude interrupted by a hesitant, almost diffident, rap upon his stateroom door. Nor, upon answering, was he particularly amazed to find himself facing Mr. Clifford Simpson. Word of disaster spreads quickly in any medium, and in the rarefied and totally encompassing atmosphere provided by a ship in transit, it speeds about even more quickly. It is extremely doubtful, at that moment, if anyone aboard the S.S. *Sunderland* was not aware that within relatively few minutes after Mrs. Penelope Watkins' hysterical shrieks had brought the master-at-arms on the run, Mr. Timothy Briggs was occupying the cell next to his friend, Mr. Carruthers, while the master-at-arms was seriously considering asking for a well-merited raise in pay.

One reason for Mr. Briggs' almost instant seizure was that, unfortunately, there was a relative dearth of tiny, wrinkled old men aboard; for another his stateroom—when the master-at-arms, now accompanied by the Captain, opened the door—stank to the gunwales with Mrs. Carpenter's particular and peculiar

scent of perfume. Nor did it take Rembrandt's talent with color
to note the similarity in shade between the orange-red on his
discarded shirt collar and the contents of the brass tube in Stateroom B-67. Plus (although this was later, after Timothy Briggs
had been properly fettered and led away) the master-at-arms, an
amateur detective at heart with the full paraphernalia of his
hobby, had unearthed loads of Mr. Briggs' fingerprints all over
the Carpenter cabin.

It didn't look good for the home team, and Clifford Simpson,
not the brightest of the triumvirate under normal circumstances,
was still sharp enough to know that now, indeed, the services of
Sir Percival Pugh were in demand. True, knowing Pugh, he
recognized the chances were good that their savings were about
to go down the drain, but he couldn't see anything else for it.
Billy-boy Carruthers up for attempted rape and Timmy Briggs
in quod for a crime demanding the high step: it certainly didn't
seem like the time to economize on defense.

Sir Percival laid aside his book and stepped back to allow his
gangling visitor to enter. The deservedly famous barrister was
a handsome, rather well-set-up gentleman in his middle forties,
slightly over middle-size in height, with an extremely sharp—if
slightly cold—pair of dark blue eyes, fair hair combed a trifle
long, and just the faintest bulge to his broad brow to indicate
the gigantic brain behind it. Once Simpson had wandered in
disconsolately and found a chair, Sir Percival closed the door
and seated himself comfortably across from his visitor. For several moments silence prevailed, until, in fact, Sir Percival
cleared his throat in a gentle reminder that they were not, after
all, in the cinema or the reading room where noise was not encouraged.

"Yes, Clifford?"

Simpson looked up unhappily. Sir Percival looked much the
same as he had during the trial when he had successfully de-
fended Simpson on a murder charge: polite, patient, and calm.

It was not surprising, since it was only a matter of months since Simpson's trial, but to the thin, tall man, it seemed like years. Trouble, he seemed to feel, could scarcely be accumulated in such quantities in so short a period. He sighed; it seemed to come from the bottom of his feet, gaining strength on its long journey to his throat.

"They didn't do it, either one, you know," he said with a touch of desperation in his voice.

"I'm quite sure they didn't," said Sir Percival. His voice remained calm, but there was a touch of sadness in it, too. He was positive his assistance was about to be requested, and since the two old gentlemen were, in his honest opinion, completely innocent, it put the famous advocate in a rather embarrassing position. Freeing the guilty was the basis upon which he had built his tremendous reputation; freeing the innocent, he had always felt, was a little like cheating. Besides, other barristers could usually free the innocent—and on occasion did—which put a severe limitation on the fees which could be charged. The guilty were always more willing to stand for a raid upon the treasury.

"Still," the famous barrister added, studying Simpson evenly, "it does seem that if your smallish friend Briggs had gone out of his way to establish a perfect picture of guilt, he could scarcely have done it better And Mr. Carruthers, apparently, has not let age bring him wisdom. I doubt if he fully appreciates the seriousness of his position."

Simpson merely nodded miserably and waited, his large eyes fixed owlishly upon the other's face.

Sir Percival sighed. "Ah, well, I suppose we'll have to get the two of them off," he said a trifle unhappily. "Can't very well let them garner the punishment they so richly deserve. . . ."

Simpson's eyes widened in sudden panic. He sat more erect.

"But I thought you said you were sure they were innocent?"

Sir Percival sighed once again. While not the equal of Simp-

son's previous sigh, it was ample to indicate his reaction to being misunderstood. Sir Percival hated to be misunderstood—
unless, of course, he was in court where being misunderstood
usually played a major part in his strategy.

"When I refer to the punishment they deserve," he said
quietly, "I mean this: Mr. Carruthers, for his ridiculous exhibition of misdirected self-esteem, particularly at his age, should be
made to go to bed without his supper for at least a week. It also
would do his figure no harm," he added absently.

"And Briggs?"

"Well, Briggs, quite obviously, was attempting to help Carruthers. Undoubtedly with your connivance. He managed entrance to the Carpenters' cabin and obviously intended to make
it appear that Mrs. Carpenter was not a monogamist in the pres-
entation of her favors. He went in, smeared lipstick all over
himself, if shipboard rumor is correct, practically drowned himself in perfume, made an unnecessarily dramatic exit—and forgot to check the bathroom while he was inside the stateroom.
When I was at law school, errors of this type were considered
Mopery with Intent to Gawk, and the punishment was usually
ten of the best applied with a cricket paddle by the strongest
member of the class—assuming, of course, that he was not the
guilty party. Such punishment, I'm afraid, can't be applied to
Briggs—although it might knock some sense into him—but it
would be quite proper to let him stew in his cell for the balance
of the trip." His eyes came up. "Unfortunately, Captain Manley-
Norville is an old friend of mine, and I cannot permit him to
open himself up to a charge of false incarceration. Which, I
might state, is lucky for Briggs."

"Yes," Simpson said, who hadn't heard a half of the diatribe,
his mind being on more pressing problems. "And to get them
off—your fee?"

For a moment the thought of the twenty thousand pounds
the three old men had received from the Jarvis-Greater-Love-

Hath-No-Man-Society award crossed Sir Percival's mind, and he recalled quite clearly his feelings on seeing the three the first day aboard. Reluctantly, however, he thrust the thought from him. To begin with, the unfortunate fact was he was sure they were innocent, which changed the picture completely. And secondly, they were in possession of something he wanted at the moment even more than money.

"Tell me," he said in his usual easy, relaxed manner—a manner known to have drawn some really remarkable confessions from some completely innocent people—"just how did you clever fellows ever manage to cheat those really quite expert card fiddlers at bridge the other day?"

For a moment Simpson failed to comprehend the sudden change in subject matter.

"Burmese solitaire," he began, and then suddenly got an unaccustomed rush of intelligence to the head. Sir Percival was a well-known bridge player at several of the more exclusive clubs. He was also known to wager large sums on the outcome. Simpson could not help but feel there might well be a connection. He leaned back, attempting to emulate Billy-boy Carruthers when he was being astute. "As I was saying," he repeated, tenting his fingers, "through an understanding of Burmese solitaire."

"Oh, ah?" Sir Percival recognized the evasion for what it was, but getting around evasions was his stock in trade. "And just what—if one might ask—is Burmese solitaire? Not to mention its connection, if any, with my question?"

Simpson was sure he was on the right track. He pictured Billy-boy sitting in his chair and answered accordingly.

"Burmese solitaire," he said in a voice that exuded sincerity, "is a game of tremendous complexity which can be learned in days or minutes, depending upon the time one has to devote to it. If the lessons gained from its knowledge are properly practiced, it enables the acolyte to win from the expert—cardsharper or not—in a great variety of games. Including, of course, bridge."

Sir Percival smiled, enjoying himself. "And just how does one go about learning to play this remarkable game? Not, I hope, by going to Burma?"

"Well," Simpson said sadly, searching his pocket for a cigar and then holding it in his fingers thoughtfully, "your question poses somewhat of a problem. You see, we are seriously thinking of putting our years of research on the subject into book form. We feel that while we can no longer write the tripe the public demands today, they will flock to buy a book on Burmese solitaire. Lines will form before shops; the police will have to be called to maintain order. That sort of thing. And, say, at five or six shillings' royalty per copy, it might well come to decent money. . . ." He was sure Billy-boy would have been proud of him. "So you can understand. . . ."

He brought a match from his pocket, scratched it into flame, applied it to his Corona and peered in friendly fashion through the smoke at Sir Percival, even as he shook the match out.

"Of course I understand," Sir Percival said, his eyes twinkling. "I also understand your fear of my fee. Let me clear away some brush: if you tell me the secret of this remarkable game, I shall see that your friends go free without any fee whatsoever. Is it agreed?"

Simpson choked over his cigar. While he had fully expected, and was prepared to accept, a reduction in the fee for information given, he had never expected the fee to be eliminated altogether. He managed to control his coughing, putting his cigar aside a moment to concentrate on the face waiting politely for his answer.

"You're serious? I have your word?"

"You have my word."

Simpson nodded, content. Sir Percival's word was his bond.

"Well, then," he said, leaning back, "Burmese solitaire is a

109

game that requires the temporary possession of all the cards on board a ship—or a train, or on the premises of a club, as the case may be. Plus, of course, a soft pencil. . . ."

Sir Percival stared at him a moment and then burst into loud laughter.

"My first thought, obviously, was that you had introduced a marked deck into the game," he said, his eyes twinkling. "I'm sure the Carpenters also thought so. However, the constant switching of decks—not at your behest, but at his—seemed to negate this possibility. How in the devil did you ever get hold of all the cards aboard ship?"

Simpson told him. Sir Percival grinned.

"And where and how are they marked?"

Simpson told him this as well. "So, you see, if the fourth port-hole in the second row is shaded, you have—"

"The jack of hearts."

"Exactly!" Simpson beamed at the barrister, as if pleased with his ready intelligence in matters unrelated to the law.

"But, fifty decks! You must have had a busy night."

"Fifty-one decks," Simpson amended, and smiled. "It really wasn't too bad, though. Just seventeen decks per person. We were lucky we weren't on the new *Queen Elizabeth*."

"You were, indeed," Sir Percival said in agreement. "I must remember to travel on small ships in the future, possibly even smaller than the S.S. *Sunderland*. Even fifty-one decks strikes me as a chore, especially for one man."

He came to his feet in an easy movement that neatly combined athletic ability with the desire to get moving.

"Well, much as I should prefer to get to the card room quickly, I suppose a bargain is a bargain. I must speak with the Captain and get his permission to visit my newly acquired clients, and then have a word with them. I suggest you go back to the bar and have a few drinks for the both of us. You might toast our success, for it is essential we get them out of pokey as quickly as possible." He smiled gently at his tall companion who was slowly unfolding himself from his chair. "I—or rather, we—are losing money every moment away from the bridge table. . . ."

Captain Charles Everton Manley-Norville had only one question to ask his old friend Sir Percival Pugh when Sir Percival came to visit him. Actually, it was eight questions, but they were really all the same question, merely put into various forms.

"Why?" he asked plaintively. "Why my ship? Why even on the same ocean? Why not the *QE2,* or better yet a freighter of Panamanian registry with a leaky hull? Why? Why didn't they go to the mountains? What curse has been laid upon me that these three Typhoid Marys, so to speak, selected the S.S. *Sunderland* for transport? Why?"

"You should learn to relax, Charles," Sir Percival advised calmly. "As I shall easily prove to your satisfaction—as well as to a jury's, should it ever come to that—these men are completely innocent of the charges against them."

"As witness the fact that you intend to defend them?" Captain Manley-Norville asked with deep sarcasm.

"Well, no," Sir Percival admitted freely. He had known the Captain for years. "Despite it, let us say."

"I'll admit they don't look the type," Captain Manley-Norville said, frowning. "And I'll admit this Carruthers insisting upon being charged with intent to rape is a bit ridiculous, but what about this Briggs? Practically caught in the act!"

"I wouldn't say that."

"You wouldn't, eh?" Captain Manley-Norville snorted. "Not only does he leave a trail that even a police inspector in a private-detective novel could follow, but he then goes up to the bar and brags in a loud voice that nearly shatters the mirror,

111

that he had—and I quote his exact words, I believe—'settled the hash of those Carpenter fiddlers.' And you consider these the words of an innocent man? Please, Percy!"

"He said that, eh? I hadn't heard that bit." Sir Percival nodded. "Mentioned settling the hash of the Carpenters, did he? And yet, to our knowledge, the hash of only one Carpenter was settled."

"I'm afraid not," said Captain Manley-Norville gloomily. He leaned forward in a burst of confidence. "I suppose I can tell you now, but Mrs. Carpenter came to me and reported her husband missing late last night. She was quite sincere, I'm sure. At first I thought it was merely a means of demanding a refund on their passage, since they had lost heavily at bridge, but the woman was truly worried. She was afraid he might have done himself harm."

Sir Percival was very interested. "And?"

"Well," said the Captain slowly, "I kept it quiet, of course, for fear of disturbing the other passengers—if he had jumped overboard and word got around, you see, it tends to upset the others—but I went to their cabin with the master-at-arms and the ship's surgeon and we made quite a search. And we found a smear of blood on the porthole sill in the main cabin. Since there was no sign that Mrs. Carpenter was near this porthole after being stabbed, I'm afraid we must look elsewhere for an explanation. And one, of course, would be that Mr. Carpenter, also bleeding, went out that porthole."

Sir Percival frowned. "Twelve hours before?"

"I know it doesn't make sense, but what does?"

Sir Percival thought a moment and then looked up.

"Tell me, Charles," he asked, "how do you square the theory that Briggs killed the two—for I assume this is in the back of your mind—with his dabbing himself about with all the lipstick and perfume? Assuming he had killed Mr. Carpenter previously, he must have come to the woman's stateroom for the express purpose of killing her for her silence. In that case, it's rather doubtful that they played fun and games first. Why, then, the putting on of the scent and color?"

"A fetish, I suppose," said the Captain gloomily. "He's from the North, you know."

"And you're sure Mr. Carpenter went through that porthole?"

"Well, nobody saw him, of course, but there is the blood. And we've had the ship searched."

"Oh, ah?"

"Yes."

"Still," Sir Percival said, "despite the overwhelming evidence —in your mind, not mine—against the man Briggs, still, he's entitled to defense."

"Why?" Captain Manley-Norville demanded.

"British justice."

"Well, I suppose so," Captain Manley-Norville said grudgingly. "Still, I wish he'd been on a French ship. They're considered guilty until proven innocent, aren't they?"

"Look at it this way," Sir Percival said in a kindly manner. "Even if the man is guilty, he might have killed another couple other than the Carpenters."

"True." The thought seemed to cheer the Captain, if only slightly. "I suppose they were the most expendable, at that. But still. . . . Well, I suppose you'll want a pass to visit them."

He came to his feet, wandered to his desk and sat down again heavily. He reached for a monogrammed piece of paper and a pen and then looked up. When he spoke his voice was almost conversational.

"I might tell you," he said, "that even if you prove the two of them innocent of all charges against them, the chances are that I shall exercise the prerogatives of my rank as Captain at sea and keep them under lock and key for the balance of the voyage. Plus their tall friend. In my opinion they should not be allowed in public on a vessel carrying nearly eight hundred souls. In my opinion, they should not be allowed loose in a rowboat on the Serpentine."

"We can wait until they have been proven innocent to discuss that phase of the problem, Charles," said Sir Percival soothingly.

"I suppose so," said the Captain. He shuddered at the thought of the threesome once again loose among the passengers, sighed deeply and proceeded to write out a pass for Sir Percival.

9

Being placed behind bars seldom has a salubrious effect upon people, and Timothy Briggs was no exception. While the hours in the brig had brought to Mr. William Carruthers a certain sense of homeliness, of belonging—although he would have been the first to admit that a painting on the wall, or even a vase of flowers, would have helped the decor— there had not been sufficient time for equal mellowness and acceptance on the part of Mr. Briggs. Still, despite this, his look as he noted Sir Percival approach along the barren, sterile corridor should have been more welcoming, for he must have realized that in Sir Percival lay his only hope of survival. However, he also realized that Sir Percival would probably not only skin them but also wrap them in plastic and put them in the fridge to keep; and being hung or skinned presented small choice to a man of the explosive temperament of Timmy Briggs.

Mr. Carruthers, however, took a more philosophical approach. To begin with, he well realized that had it not been for the efforts of Sir Percival Pugh, his good friend Clifford Simpson would have suffered either the hangman's noose or the booby hatch a few months before. Besides, Billy-boy Carruthers had always been one to whom the motto "Watch and Wait" offered a modicum, if not a magnum, of hope. There was also the reassuring fact, of course, that the arrangement of their joint account did not permit Simpson to hand over all their cash to Sir Percival even if a mistaken sense of loyalty made him wish to. This gave some slight hope that after the debacle enough might be left over to keep them from the poor farm for several weeks, at least.

Since both the quantity and quality of crime aboard the S.S. *Sunderland* had increased so impressively, the master-at-arms was now present at the scene in the role of warder. This gentleman was a suspicious-looking smallish man named by unthinking parents James Vincent King, and years of filling out forms of one type and another—for school, for the dole, and on rare occasions for employment—as King, James V., had done little to improve his bias toward a human race that seemed to think it comical to bow to him upon introduction.

He came up from his stool as if prepared for physical attack, took the Captain's pass from Sir Percival, studied it cautiously for several moments, his lips moving painfully, and then reluctantly moved down the corridor out of earshot, giving the barrister unrestricted access to his clients. James V. King did not move so far, however, that he could not instantly have noted any attempt on the part of Sir Percival to smuggle a hacksaw blade hidden in a chocolate cake through the bars. As Mr. King would have been the first to tell you, he was far from the complete fool he appeared.

"Well, well! Mr. Carruthers!" Sir Percival beamed genially at the occupant of the cell to the right. "You're looking quite fit, I must say."

Mr. Carruthers smiled back in friendly enough style, although he refused at the moment to commit himself to words for which

he might later be sorry. He was a great believer in the Nor-
wegian proverb that a shut mouth catches no reindeer, and he
felt that in his present position this was as good a time as any to
practice the dictates of Scandinavian philosophy.

"And Mr. Briggs." Sir Percival turned to the second cell, not
at all disturbed by the lack of communication from the first.
"You're keeping well, I trust?"

"Grrraaagh!" said Briggs, more vocal than Carruthers.

"The food is adequate, I imagine?"

"Grrraaagh!"

"Yes. As you say. Well, gentlemen," said Sir Percival, drawing
up the warder's stool and seating himself, "much as I should
like to continue this friendly chat indefinitely, I'm afraid time
does not permit. I suggest we get down to business. You are both
in somewhat of a hole, I'm afraid, and your individual stories
would do much to entertain me. And possibly even point a possible way for your defense. Shall we start with you, Mr. Carruthers—?"

"No! Let's start with me!" Briggs said with a black scowl on
his tiny face. His small hands clutched the bars fiercely. "And
the first thing I want to know is how much nicker you think
you're going to stick us for?"

Sir Percival was not at all pained by this approach. It was
quite common among his clientele, and particularly among
those who were forced to deal with him more than once.

"Please, Mr. Briggs. To begin with, all arrangements for the
payment of my fee have been concluded. Through Mr. Simpson, I might add." He looked at the small occupant of the second cell quite calmly. "I might also add that he seemed to
handle the arrangements with a bit less emotion than you tend
to display."

"Oh, he did, did he? Well, let me tell you—!"

"Tim!" Mr. Carruthers' voice was sharp with disapproval.
"You are being impolite. Sir Percival is here to help us. Besides,

Cliff is in no position to make commitments for us, least of all financial commitments."

Briggs was not satisfied. "But he said—"

"Unless," Carruthers continued, quite as if he had not been interrupted, "the payment was other than money?"

The famous barrister nodded pleasantly. "As a matter of fact, you're quite right."

"What is this?" Briggs demanded suspiciously.

"Burmese solitaire," Carruthers explained gently, turning to the occupant of the adjoining cell. "You see, Tim, Sir Percival is in rather an awkward spot. Being innocent, we present him with a certain problem in defending us. However, he can ease his conscience somewhat by accepting, in lieu of money, the secret of our success at the bridge table. I am happy and proud," he added, turning back to their guest, "—and also a bit surprised—that Cliff had the brains to see it."

Sir Percival smiled at Carruthers with true appreciation.

"I am amazed, Mr. Carruthers," he said, "that a man capable of analyzing a situation as correctly as you have just done should still permit his ego to lead him into the embarrassing situation that you did vis-à-vis Mrs. Carpenter and her charms."

"Do you mean," Briggs interrupted, still unable to credit his ears, "that knowing how the playing cards are marked aboard this tub is worth more to you than money? You? Sir Percival?" He turned to the other cell. "Billy-boy! Call the master-at-arms! This man is an obvious imposter!"

"Quiet, Tim!" Mr. Carruthers' glare drove the smaller man to a sullen silence. Billy-boy returned his attention to the barrister. "I agree, Sir Percival, that it was rather a bad mistake on my part, dictated by a whim of the moment. But with the lady dead, I'm afraid it's a bit late for denials."

"For the usual ones, I suppose," Sir Percival said in agreement. "I could probably come up with five or six explanations that would satisfy a jury, if need be, but let us hope it does not come to that." His pleasant look faded a bit as he took the two men into his confidence. "However, there are several rather unusual problems connected with your defense. Normally, of course, in a murder case where the victim is married, the spouse —wife or husband as the case may be—is almost immediately suspected, almost invariably charged, and in an inordinately high precentage of cases is found guilty of the crime. Unless, of course," he added in the interests of honesty, "I defend them. In the case of the Carpenters, however—"

"Of course! I'm an idiot!" Billy-boy Carruthers was disgusted with himself for having forgotten this first precept of crime detection. "How could I ever have come to overlook such an obvious fact? Other, of course," he added, thinking about it, "that in a mystery novel it would be too easy. Yes—" A touch of enthusiasm entered his rich voice. "Mr. Carpenter would make an excellent suspect! Loads of oil on his hair, that villainous mustache, that sneaky look—"

"He isn't as sneaky as that nosy steward who turned me in!" Briggs grumbled, scowling. "That's the bloody spiv I'd like to see charged with the murder!"

"That's scarcely fair," Carruthers reminded the man in the next cell. "After all, you went to a great deal of trouble to make sure he would see you and pass the word along. Well, didn't you?"

"Grrraaagh!" replied Briggs.

"However," Sir Percival continued equably, not a bit upset— or influenced—by the interruptions, "as I was saying, in the case of the Carpenters there is an added factor. Mr. Carpenter, it seems, is missing, and had been for at least twelve hours before his wife's demise. And there appears to be evidence in the form of a bloodstain on the porthole sill in their stateroom that leads the Captain to believe he left the ship through this somewhat unorthodox exit. Obviously, it appears, with someone's contrivance."

Mr. Carruthers shook his head pityingly.

"No, no!" There was a disparaging note in his voice. "I can tell you all about that!" He proceeded to do so. "It was the old chicken bladder swindle; you must have heard of it. Goes back years and years. Chap pretends he's been shot by someone philandering with his wife. Falls down, writhes about a bit looking gruesome, bites on a small bag of chicken blood he's been hiding in his cheek, and then dramatically expires, bleeding all over the place from the mouth. The wife hustles the mark out of the room instanter, and later, of course, the poor idiot is jam on toast for blackmail."

"You mean—?"

"Exactly. That's chicken blood on the porthole sill. Mr. Artful Dodger Carpenter carried the farce out to the bitter end. I have to give him credit." His bright blue eyes suddenly twinkled in memory. "You see, I very nearly had him out the porthole before our sneaky-looking friend suddenly decided he didn't want to be a corpse after all. Figured he hadn't been shot, by some miracle."

There were several seconds of silence while Sir Percival took this added factor into account, feeding it into the computer bank of his brain. A bit down the hall King, James V. hunkered down against the wall, picking his teeth with a broom straw and watching closely for any attempt on the part of the barrister-type, lord or no, to smuggle dynamite into the cell for the purposes of blowing it up and freeing the miscreants. He had once read such a plot in an old book found in his grandfather's attic; he would have been amazed—and even more watchful—had he known it had been written by none other than the portly gentleman in Cell No. 1.

Sir Percival nodded slowly as he looked up.

"Excellent," he said. "There is therefore the possibility that the Carpenters, failing in their attempt to get money from you, tried the same trick on someone else after you had been dragged off to choky. And the other party may not have been as easily dissuaded at the last moment from putting a blackmailer through a porthole. . . ."

Carruthers nodded in agreement, wondering that he had not thought of it himself. Briggs merely watched owlishly from the adjoining cell. Sir Percival carried on.

"Add to this possibility the fact that—prior to you—the Carpenters had cheated four or five couples substantially at the bridge table, and—" He smiled encouragingly. "Just think; almost anyone aboard this ship is a potential suspect."

"Great!" Briggs said sourly. "Is that supposed to reassure us?"

"It's usually considered somewhat better than being the *only* suspect," Sir Percival pointed out, and then added, both for the sake of honesty and because Briggs was beginning to faintly irk even this paragon of patience, "Of course, the others weren't caught practically red-handed. . . ."

Briggs glowered but, for the time being at least, remained silent. Sir Percival returned to business.

"All right. Now I'd like to hear your stories. Not, of course, that it makes much difference . . . "

"I beg your pardon?" Carruthers was staring at him.

"Never mind. Your stories, please. Complete in all detail, as truthful as you feel necessary considering the slightest lie can hang you, and leaving out as many unnecessary adjectives, adverbs and expletives as possible. Mr. Carruthers? Let's start with you."

The next half hour or so was spent in detailing a full history of the relationship between the three founding members of the Mystery Authors Club and the Carpenters, male and female. Sir Percival took no written notes but allowed the statements to be engraven upon his tremendous memory word by word, even as his giant intellect made sense out of them. When at last he had dragged the final comma and semicolon from the pair, he nodded optimistically and came to his feet, straightening the creases in his trousers. Another barrister, facing the facts as they had been presented, might well have quailed at the thought of attempting a defense based upon them, but the idea of failure never crossed Sir Percival's mind.

"A fairly simple problem, really," he said in an offhand manner, and prepared to depart.

"Simple?" Briggs exclaimed.

"Why, yes." Sir Percival smiled at him brightly.

But Billy-boy Carruthers had a far more important question in mind.

"Just what did you mean a while ago," he asked curiously, "when you said you wanted to hear our stories, and then you added, 'Not that it makes much difference'?"

"Just what you heard," Sir Percival said calmly and prepared to waste a few more minutes in the interest of educating his clients. "After all, we do have a wealth of potential suspects, do we not? I certainly don't intend the facts as you've stated them to be allowed to interfere with my defense." He shrugged. "As I said, simple. We pick a likely suspect from our endless group and accuse him of the crime. If driven to it, I suppose, I could even prove him guilty, though let's hope it doesn't come to that."

"How?" Carruthers demanded. "If he didn't do it?"

"How do I know? It's early on." Sir Percival glanced at his watch and smiled in their general direction. "Well, ta. Time for work."

"Wait! Wait!" Carruthers looked at the famous barrister aghast. "You mean you'd accuse an innocent man just to free us?"

"Well, you do want to be freed, don't you?"

"Not under such circumstances! I won't hear of it!"

"Now, if it was that sneaky steward—" Briggs began thoughtfully.

"Tim! Quiet! Sir Percival—"

But Sir Percival had raised a hand for silence.

"You know," he said slowly, "that really isn't a bad idea. The idea of the steward, you know. Being British he'd be returned to England as a matter of course; and if you're really worried about his suffering for something he didn't do, why, I'd defend him." He looked at Carruthers evenly. "I've never lost a case, you know."

"And who would pay?" Briggs demanded.

"Why, I suppose you would," Sir Percival said, and smiled.

Briggs shook his head decisively. "Forget the steward!"

"Now see here!" Carruthers said firmly, "I refuse to stand by and have an innocent man accused of murder just in order to save my own neck. Both Tim and I are innocent; that should be sufficient." He disregarded Sir Percival's look of astonished pity. "You'll simply have to find some other means of defense."

Sir Percival sighed and shook his head sadly.

"You make it dashed difficult, you know. Normally, I don't listen to clients in the course of charting a defense, but I suppose your being innocent makes a difference. And I can't drop the case or refuse it because I've already been paid and can't return the fee. The devil!" He looked up bravely. "Well, we'll come up with something; we always have. If anything further occurs to you, be in touch. I suppose the master-at-arms will carry a message; you can't very well wrap it in a brick and toss it out the window. In the meantime, ta. Patience and faith. And worry not; the truth shall set you free!"

With a brief wave of a manicured hand he turned and moved off down the corridor, pausing only long enough to advise King, James V. that his throne could once again be occupied. Behind him Carruthers was still in partial shock from the barrister's naughty suggestion.

"I knew he was a twister," he said, "but can you imagine? Accusing an innocent man? Even if he got him off later, think of the shock, of the shame? Of the time in quod?" He turned to

123

get Briggs' reaction to his impassioned statement and then frowned at the expression on the other's face. "What's the matter with you?"

"Now I'm really worried!" Briggs said darkly.

"What about?"

"You heard him say 'The truth shall set you free,' didn't you? Well," Briggs said heavily, "the day old Pugh has to fall back on the truth, we're sunk!"

"My dear Simpson," Sir Percival exclaimed, exhibiting his normal patience once again. "It wasn't my first or my best plan, in the first place. If it weren't for the completely incomprehensible attitude of your two friends, we'd be home free. But since I had to come up with an alternate scheme—and did—it seems to me that a bit less objection on your part would be in order."

He was beginning to feel the room had an echo, for he had been repeating the same statement in one form or another for some time. The two men were seated at the corner table in the Promenade Deck bar, partaking of brandy and champagne. While it was a new drink to Sir Pervical, he had taken to it instantly. He only wished that Simpson's reaction to his scheme had been accepted with the same alacrity.

"I know it wasn't your first scheme," Simpson said stubbornly and dug a cigar from his pocket. He lit it broodingly and tossed away the match. "But it isn't much more honest. It's cheating, and while that's better than sending a man over who's innocent, it's still cheating."

Sir Percival stared at him. "And taking nearly three thousand pounds from the Carpenters using a marked deck was not?"

"But that was different, you see," Simpson explained. He put aside his cigar long enough to sample his drink and then put his drink aside in order to sample his cigar. It was evident he was using the time to put his thoughts in order. "Billy-boy Carruthers explained it all to us, you see. It seems there was—or is, for all I know—this poor American author, brilliant in some ways, but an absolute sod in others, and he—"

He proceeded to repeat the sad tale of the book club in the States who had refused to handle the history of the Murder League simply because the naughty boys had profited from their crime.

"So you can understand," Simpson ended, "why we have to avoid any hanky-panky. Billy-boy wouldn't stand for it. The same reason he miffed on the accusing-of-innocents bit. You see?"

"You were saying something about cheating the Carpenters—"

"Oh, yes! I forgot. Billy-boy felt that taking a pair of card cheats was sort of the old Biter-Bit thing, you know. He felt this book club wouldn't—or anyway, shouldn't—be too upset about that."

"In that case," said Sir Percival—for his mammoth brain had instantly seen the opportunity presented and jumped upon it —"if the Biter-Bit is acceptable, how much more acceptable Justice Triumphant?"

"I beg your pardon?"

"I mean, it appears that if my normal means of operation have been denied me, I must actually discover the guilty party. This is known, in case you've missed TV lately, as Justice Triumphant."

"But must we cheat to do it?"

There were several seconds of silence while Sir Percival reminded himself that he had made a bargain and that he had never gone back on his word in his life. He also reminded himself that if anyone could solve the contretemps of the echo, it was he, himself, Sir Percival Pugh. He stared across the table hypnotically, much as he eyed witnesses for the prosecution.

"May we take it step by step once more?"

"Of course." Simpson was ever the gentleman.

"Now, someone killed either one or two of the Carpenters. Right?"

"Right."

"We are in agreement that neither Carruthers nor Briggs, solely or in partnership, are guilty of the crime or crimes. Right?"

"Eminently right."

"Therefore—ergo—the criminal or criminals had to be others. Right?"

"Everything's fine so far."

"Good. If I lose you anywhere down the line, merely raise your hand." Sir Percival took a breath and continued. "Now: it is reasonable to assume that whoever killed the Carpenter or Carpenters did not do so out of idle whim or fancy, but had a reason for so doing. Right?"

"Very logical. I mean, right."

"Thank you. Now, since the Carpenter family included in their repertoire both card tricks as well as blackmail, it is reasonable to assume that it was precisely these nefarious practices that might well have played a major part in inducing their killers to eliminate them. Right?"

Simpson frowned. "I'm afraid you lost me somewhere back there."

Sir Percival was not at all perturbed. Whenever he allowed rhetoric to sweep him along it happened quite frequently.

"Let me put it to you this way: is it not reasonable to assume that the Carpenters might have cheated someone who resented it and that resentment was expressed by killing them?"

Simpson nodded, seeing the light.

"Right!" He recognized the word as being inappropriate and made the proper correction. "I mean, yes. It is. Reasonable, that is."

"Fine! Now," said Sir Percival, leaning forward, his glittering eye holding the other in a manner the Ancient Mariner would have envied, "as I mentioned to your friends in the dungeon below, there are four or five couples on board whom I have seen playing with the Carpenters, and whom I have seen lose large sums to these same Carpenters. Fortunately, lacking a partner whose game I know, I never managed to get involved."

"Right! I mean, if you say so."

"I do say so." The famous barrister paused for emphasis. "Now, then: my plan is simplicity itself. You and I as partners will play with these four or five—or six—couples, one at a time, of course, and we shall cheat them as openly as we can without having them get up and walk away, or, conversely, stay and slap our faces. Do you understand?"

"Right! I mean, well, not quite."

"If I finish you may see the dawn." Sir Percival glanced through the windows of the bar and sighed. "We may both very well see the dawn. But no matter. Let me carry on. We want to cheat them so they know they're being cheated. Do you understand?"

"No." Simpson frowned. "What's the point?"

Sir Percival sighed once again. He reminded himself of the years he had spent building up his reputation as a man impossible to disturb, as a rock in a sea of vacillating advocates, all of whom easily lost their tempers and panicked at the first sign of adversity.

"It is generally conceded," he said at last, "that having committed one murder, your normal killer hesitates not at all at committing a second. It rather becomes routine, if you see what I mean. The one who killed the Carpenters for cheating wouldn't have the slightest compunction in killing the next one who cheated. *Now* do you see?"

"Oh, ah! Now I see! Brilliant!" Simpson smiled all over his face. "And I'm sure it would get by Billy-boy's infernal sense of propriety, as well. We only cheat the killers to get them to try and kill us, eh? Make them uncover their hand, so to speak, what? An excellent idea! Make them blot their copybook, eh?"

For once Sir Percival had a chance to respond to a question.

"Right!"

"And if they kill us, of course," Simpson charged on, his brain clicking furiously, "why, we've got them, what?" He paused as his own words came back to him. "By the way, what about that angle, eh? Have you considered it at sufficient length? Their killing us, I mean?"

"I hadn't thought of carrying our experiment to quite that degree of thoroughness," Sir Percival said gently. "I thought that once we had a good idea who the killer or killers were, we might bow out of the picture, giving our information to the Captain. Let him carry on. As long as Carruthers and Briggs were freed. . . ."

"Oh, ah! Of course, of course! It wouldn't do to be victims ourselves, would it? Lose the whole point of the thing." One final question occurred to Simpson. "What about the proceeds?"

"The proceeds?"

"Well, if we cheat, we'll be bound to win, won't we?"

Sir Percival stared across the table in silence for several moments. Simpson leaned forward.

"Well, we will, won't we? It wouldn't make much sense if we lost, would it? Couldn't very well trap anyone that way, could we?"

"No, we couldn't." Sir Percival sighed deeply as he considered the question. He had hoped that this point would have been overlooked by his tall companion, but apparently it hadn't. "For the purposes of this demonstration," he said sadly, "and if you feel that strongly about it, the proceeds of our first gambling venture can be donated to the Seaman's Fund, I suppose."

"Oh, I don't think we have to go as far as all that," Simpson said hastily. He sipped his drink and then looked up, his eyes gauging his companion. "I imagine splitting them right down the line would serve the purpose just as well. After all, as you said, it *is* all in the cause of Justice. . . ."

10

Mr. Clifford Simpson, dispatched by Sir Percival Pugh to the card room adjacent to the main salon in order to locate primary targets for their unfortunately necessary chicanery, returned in an inordinately short time, his long face even longer. Sir Percival frowned as he watched the thin man fold himself unhappily along one side of the wide chair and reach for the Corona he had left smoldering in an ash tray to one side.

"What's the trouble?"

Simpson shook his head dejectedly. Freeing his friends was proving more of a problem than he had anticipated.

"The women are having something called a canasta tournament. No bridge today."

"Oh?" Sir Percival was disappointed. The urge to put his knowledge of Burmese solitaire into use, while not overwhelming—since nothing exactly overwhelmed him—was still strong. "What's canasta?"

"Some form of rummy as far as I could tell, just giving it a quick glance in passing," Simpson said disconsolately. "I think it's a Spanish game, or something. Something to do with baskets."

Sir Percival was quite ready to agree with this.

"Yes. Only a basket would have blocked our bridge game to-day." His one hand brought his glass to his lips; the fingers of the other hand, remarkably independent in operation, drummed the table in irritable restlessness at this hiatus in their schedule.

"Yes," said Simpson, and sighed. He puffed his cigar a few moments, bringing it back to life, and then remembered something else. He tossed it in more to keep the conversation from flagging than for any other reason. "Can't even get up a bridge game with the men."

"No? Why? What are they playing? Squat tag?"

"No," said Simpson. "They're over in the other corner of the card room playing poker."

Sir Percival, in the act of swallowing a bit of his champagne, coughed and sprayed a fair quantity in the general area. A waiter, eyeing him coldly, arrived and wiped about a bit with a towel, after which he removed himself, shaking his head. Sir Percival put aside his glass and stared at Simpson as if wondering how the doddering old idiot had ever managed to get through this vale of tears without a keeper well equipped with handkerchiefs.

"Poker?" he said sarcastically. "And you didn't consider this fact important enough to mention earlier? Let's go. Poker is even better for our purpose than bridge."

"Except that I don't play poker," Simpson said sadly.

Sir Percival, who had been in the act of rising ready to trot down the deck to the card room, settled back again, reaching for his glass. He poured himself a fair dollop and looked up.

"Well," he said, "fortunately, I do. And you will, in about five minutes, which is as long as it would take a three-year-old child, not unduly retarded, to learn the game. Knowing the cards as well as we do, I should judge a two year old could handle the job after a bad head injury." He leaned forward, concentrating on his tutoring task. "The game is played by any

number up to seven, generally, although there are forms which,
since they involve the use of fewer cards per player, can allow
an even greater number to play. The exact form of the game
played each hand is usually chosen by the dealer. Is that clear?"

"No," Simpson replied honestly.

"No, I suppose not. Well, let's let that go by for the nonce.
Let's stick with the vital statistics, shall we? The game is played
with five cards per player, although in some forms these five are
selected from seven, while in other forms these five are made up
of the number you hold the first time around plus whatever
number you take to make up for the ones you discard." He studied his companion anxiously. "How did we score on that one?"

"Completely bowled out," Simpson admitted unhappily.

"Well," said Sir Percival, reviewing his own words, "I can't
say that I blame you. Let me see. . . ." He drummed his fingers
a moment and then decided to try a simpler version. "Look; the
chances are they will play one of two forms: draw or stud. In
draw poker the dealer deals five cards to each player; they se-
lect the ones they want to keep and discard the balance. After
a round of betting that is. At this point the dealer proceeds to
give each player enough cards to bring his total back to five, at
which point everyone bets once more. Is *that* clear?"

"As far as it goes. But on what basis does one hold or discard
cards?"

"We'll come to that. Now; the other form is stud poker. Here
one card is dealt face downward to each player and another then
dealt face upward. The betting then begins, after which a second card is dealt to each player face up. There is alternate betting and dealing until each player has five cards, when the final
bets are made. Clear?"

"I believe so. But what about spit-in-the-ocean and one-eyed
jacks?"

Sir Percival stared at him. "Where did you even *hear* those
terms?"

"Mrs. Carpenter mentioned them when she asked if we played poker."

"Well, forget them. Spit-in-the-ocean!" Sir Percival sounded as if whatever fate had overtaken Mrs. Carpenter was deserved for even faintly considering playing the game. "In any event, if any form of the game is chosen by the dealer other than stud or draw, you merely sit out that hand."

"Right-O."

"Good. Now let's get down to brass tacks. You do know what a pair is, don't you?"

"Of course," Simpson said, happy that they were speaking the same language once again.

"I'm pleased. Well, add one to a pair—the same number of pips, of course—and you have what is known as three of a kind."

"I must say," Simpson said, intrigued, "it sounds quite logical."

"Yes. Descartes would have reveled in it, and, for all I know, he did. Where were we? Oh, yes. To continue; if you happen to hold all four of any card, you have what is known in the trade as four of a kind." He peered across the table. "Can you follow that line of thought?"

"Quite."

"Fine," said Sir Percival with satisfaction. "You see? Scarcely thirty seconds and you have fully half the game at your complete command. Now, let's move along, shall we?"

"Carry on," Simpson said bravely.

"I shall. Well, the next thing I suppose you ought to remember is that, contrary to bridge, one suit has no particular precedence over another. That is, spades are no more valuable than clubs. However, if one should hold all five cards in the same suit, one has what is known as a flush." He saw the frown beginning to crease Simpson's forehead. "I say, why don't you try repeating some of these things after me, just to fix them in your head, eh?"

"Five cards in the same suit constitute a flush."

"You see? I told you. Any three-year-old. . . . Now; a sequence of cards—say a six, seven, eight, nine and ten, or any other sequence regardless of the suit of each card, is called a straight. And for the purposes of poker, the ace can be either high or low; either beginning the smallest straight, or ending the highest. Got that? Five in a row, like Mrs. Carey's something-or-others—or was it Mrs. Wiggs? Well, no matter." He beamed expectantly at his pupil. "I say, why not try it for echo, eh?"

Simpson obediently tried it for echo. "A sequence of five cards is called a straight."

"Excellent!" Sir Percival was pleased and showed it. "Naturally, under these circumstances, a sequence of five cards in the *same* suit would be called—?"

"A flushed straight?"

"A reasonable assumption, but—like so many reasonable assumptions—wrong, I'm afraid. A straight flush."

"A straight flush."

There was a moment's silence while Sir Percival put down his glass and studied the man across from him evenly.

"You see?" he said. "That's the entire game of poker. I told you; extremely simple. I shouldn't be at all surprised if, upon returning to London, you might not even set up as an instructor in the game to those who lack your knowledge." He started to come to his feet. "Well, let's go. There are worlds to conquer. To pluralize Robert Frost, 'For we have promises to keep, and miles to go before we sleep.' "

"But I still don't know the value of one hand against another," Simpson objected.

"Oh." Sir Percival sank down again. "Yes, I overlooked mentioning that, didn't I?" He withdrew a pencil from a pocket, turned over a napkin and commenced writing in his neat fist. "Well, as to the value of the hands, I'll set them down in ascending order for you. There's no rule against having a table of comparative values at your elbow while you're playing."

Simpson watched in owlish admiration as Sir Percival went down the list; as he wrote the baronet repeated himself under his breath.

"One pair, two pair—two pairs, actually, if one wishes to be grammatically correct—then three of a kind, followed in order by a straight, then a flush, after which we have a full house—"

"A what?"

Sir Percival looked up. "A full house. Didn't I enunciate?"

"What's a full house?"

Sir Percival appeared more interested than upset.

"Did I forget that, too? Oh, dear. Well, I suppose I did. I'll have to revise that estimate of a three-year-old to a four-year-old at this rate. In any event, a full house is a three of a kind together with a pair in the same hand. If two players each have full houses (or would it be fulls house, like cups? No, I suppose not), then the player with the three of a kind with the higher value wins. The pair has nothing to do with the value of a full house. Is that clear?"

"Perfectly."

"Good," said Sir Percival, relieved. "Then please don't interrupt anymore." He returned to his listing. "Where was I? Oh, yes: a full house, then four of a kind, a straight flush and finally a royal flush, the higher the better. And you're home free."

He finished his writing, put his pencil back into his jacket pocket with a slight flourish and handed over the napkin. Simpson accepted it gratefully.

"Thank you."

"My pleasure." Sir Percival placed his hands upon the tabletop, preparatory to pushing himself erect, and then paused in surprise at the woebegone expression on Simpson's face. "*Now,* what's the trouble?"

"I don't know the first thing about betting—" Simpson

squared his shoulders, confident that his complaint was a just one. "After all, I don't believe I can be caught cheating—which is the object, remember—by simply watching others play. Unless, of course, they are also cheating. In bridge it was quite simple to cheat the Carpenters, but in a new game with all types of odd hands and inverted values. . . ."

Sir Percival smote himself on the brow.

"It must be the sea air. I remember being taken to Brighton as a child and not being able to manage the penny machine without a penny, a problem I never faced back home in London."

"The betting," Simpson reminded him.

"Of course. I apologize for the oversight. Well," said Sir Percival, "it works like this: if you have a higher value hand than your opponent—or opponents, as the case may be—you place a wager to the limit that the game is being played for. If you consistently wager the maximum and win, this of itself will cast suspicion upon you. However, after your bet, the others may do one of three things: either drop out of the play and admit defeat, in which case you pick up the money; or they may choose to meet your wager, in which case you compare cards and the higher value hand—in this case, invariably yourself— will win; or thirdly, they may exhibit excessive cooperation with our purposes and not only meet the wager but even raise it."

"Raise it? What does that mean?"

"I was about to come to that," Sir Percival said a trifle chidingly. "They may place an amount of money equal to your wager upon the table and then add a sum of money to it. This extra sum is called a raise. In this case you will meet this extra wager and add, yourself, the maximum amount permitted by the rules of the game. This merry chase continues until your opponent begins to suspect that he may not, truly, have the best hand. At this time he will merely call you."

He saw Simpson open his mouth and hastened to define the new term.

"By calling, I mean he will merely meet your wager. At which time—"

"We turn over our cards and I pick up the money."

"Precisely," Sir Percival said, and beamed. His beam faded somewhat as he considered his partner-in-crime across the table. "What we have been discussing, of course," he added, "is totally dependent upon your betting when you know you have the better hand. You *do* know how to read the backs of those cards, don't you?"

"Of course. I told you. Top row of portholes, spades. Second row—"

Sir Percival interrupted. "And the value of the poker hands is clear in your mind? Although, even during the play of a hand, you may freely refer to your napkin if you wish."

"I know. There's just one thing, though—"

Sir Percival, who had been in the act of rising for the fourth time, fell back once again. He was beginning to feel like a toy condemned to a rocking action forever, or until its spring ran down.

"What is it this time?"

"Well, suppose I don't have the best hand?"

Sir Percival stared at him.

"Then, quite obviously, you do not play that hand. You drop your cards as if they were aflame. You leave yourself out of the action. Is that clear?"

"Oh, ah! Don't have to play them all, eh?"

"No," said Sir Percival heavily, "You do not have to play them all."

"Good-O." There was a moment's silence while Sir Percival waited; he was sure Simpson would think of something else. He was not mistaken. "But are you sure they'll suspect cheating?"

"Let me put it to you this way," Sir Percival said. "If I sat down with a beginner at the game of poker—and a beginner who had a napkin with a list of values he constantly referred to—

and he bet the maximum each time he stayed in a hand, and he won every hand he played—well, I'm afraid I should seriously suspect that the theory of probabilities was receiving help from someone; and not being a particularly religious man, I'm afraid I wouldn't accept divine assistance as the answer."

He started to his feet and then sank down again. This time, however, the fault was his own. One thing needed to be said that had not been said.

"By the way, I intend to play so that you are the winner in any hand possible. In other words, if a hand comes down to myself and you, I shall drop out and allow you to win, whether my hand is better or not. Is that clear?"

"Quite," Simpson said, and he suddenly looked across the table with a shrewdness Sir Percival had not suspected. "No sense in having any potential killers chasing after two victims, is there?"

For several minutes Sir Percival returned the even stare of the other, and then he came to his feet. Years of experience had taught him never to lie when it was unnecessary.

"Quite," he said, and moved toward the door leading from the bar.

The four men sitting around the poker table in the northwest corner of the card room off the Main Salon were having a hard time of it. The screams of delight mixed with the despairing shrieks of woe eminating from the southeast corner; the clangor of recipes being exchanged intermingled with the bewildered cries of "Whose turn is it to play?"—in short, the usual racket produced by five women gathered anywhere at any time for any occasion was hard to bear. Add to this the fact that originally there had been five players in the poker game but one man had dropped out preferring—he said—to go down to the engine room and get some peace and quiet, and the attitude of the men at the table can be understood.

Four players do not a poker game make, or at least not the type of game these men preferred, so the sight of Simpson and Sir Percival approaching brought hope to the hearts of the four. Even the women seemed to reduce their racket a decibel or two at sight of the famous barrister. Sir Percival stood behind one man and smiled genially about the group.

"Room for two more?"

"A pleasure." The words were bounced about the table, the tone in most cases genuinely hospitable.

"Absolute duffers, you know."

"All the better," said one, a pleasant-faced man named Wilkins, raking in the chips at the moment. The others smiled at the mot.

"Good-O, then," said Sir Percival and drew up a chair. Simpson took a place well separated from his co-conspirator, while the man at his left—a huge man named Marmaduke Montmorency, who looked as if he had not only been forced to fight daily to defend his name but had come to enjoy it (the fighting, not the name)—turned and called to the library steward in a harsh voice.

"New blood calls for a new deck, Steward."

He gathered up the old deck and pushed the cards aside. Sir Percival picked them up, checking the backs to see if his memory was in order and then, reassured that it was, put them on an adjoining table. The sextet waited patiently while the steward disappeared into the library to return a moment later and place a packet on the table.

"You can shuffle and deal," said the huge man, pushing the new deck toward Simpson. "New man and all that, you know." He made it sound much more a command than a request. One finger thick as a sausage pushed the deck before Simpson. The tiny hard eyes of the huge fellow peered at Simpson accusingly. "What's your game?"

Simpson swallowed; he could feel himself getting pale.

138

"My game?" He forced sincerity into his voice. "Believe me, sir, I merely wanted to play some poker. I assure you there was no ulterior motive behind it at all. . . ."

The other men at the table laughed with enjoyment at the clever response to the age-old question, but the huge man did not seem to find it all that comical. His bushy eyebrows rose dangerously.

"Oh, a joker, eh?"

"Is that like a one-eyed jack? Because I don't play with wild cards." There was a touch of pride in Simpson's voice; he had not forgotten.

Sir Percival thought it time to intervene.

"The gentleman was simply asking which particular form of poker you intend to deal, Clifford."

"Oh!" Simpson smiled in embarrassment. He placed his napkin in plain view, picked up the deck and sliced the seal while thinking. He looked about, pleased to have arrived at a decision. "I say, how about a round of stallion?"

"Stallion?" asked Mr. Wilkins.

"Yes. I'm sure you all must be familiar with it; I understand it's one of the more common forms of the game. One places one card face downward before each player and then deals the balance of the hand with the faces of the cards open for inspection."

The laughter returned, sweeping the table. This Simpson was really a card!

"I think you mean stud," said Mr. Wilkins.

"Do I?" Simpson concentrated and then nodded. "Yes, of course. I'm sorry." He smiled in friendly fashion, pleased that he had amused the others, even if unwittingly. Even Sir Percival seemed pleased; the true reason being, of course, that nobody had ever given such a poor performance before. Winning was bound to set Simpson off as the most inept card cheat of all times.

Only the huge Mr. Montmorency didn't appear to be entertained. His grating voice jarred through the laughter. "Deal!"

"Oh. Of course. Sorry."

Simpson slipped the cards from the deck face upward, removed the two jokers and began to shuffle them. A few riffles in this position and he turned them over. Suddenly he blanched; his eyes rose in horror.

"What's the matter?" Mr. Wilkins asked in a tone of concern.

"I do believe I'm going to be sick," said Simpson in a small voice, and meant it.

Sir Percival glanced across the table and then cast his eyes toward the ceiling in supplication. Before Simpson the cards did not exhibit the S.S. *Sunderland* with its neat four rows of portholes; the backs of these cards showed a gaily colored bird leaning dangerously from the limb of a lush tree in some exotic glade. . . .

11

"The ruddy library steward said—" Simpson changed his tone of voice, raising it slightly, giving a fair imitation of the prissy voice of the steward. " 'The Captain had some extra decks in his digs—private like, sir—and he told me to offer them in case you, Mr. Simpson, wished to play cards. I had no idea he had them, sir, but wasn't that thoughtful of him? And those birds; my, aren't they pretty? Don't you think so, sir?' No," Simpson went on, resuming his normal tone, "I didn't think them pretty!"

"The Captain, eh?" Carruthers looked thoughtful. "I had a cold feeling in the pit of my stomach that our uniformed Charon wasn't as stupid as he looked." He sighed and shook his head. "What did Pugh say? And where is he, by the way?"

"He didn't say anything," Simpson said. "After I excused myself from the game, he stayed on, playing. Picked up the cards, shuffled them right smartly, and dealt them." He glanced at his wristwatch. "The game ought to be breaking up soon, though. Getting on toward lunch time, you know."

"That's our bloody barrister for you," Briggs said with bitter accusation from the adjoining cell. "Here we are in the bloody brig and he's off playing bloody cards."

"He may still learn something, though, you know," Simpson said with a thoughtful frown. "I watched for a few moments and he seemed to hold the deck in the same fashion as that Carpenter chap. You know, fingers curled around the edge of the deck? And Pugh won the first three hands in a row. . . ."

"Oh, ah?" Carruthers smiled brightly. "You may be right. He may still learn something from the game."

"Cheating, eh?" said Briggs with fine illogic, and sniffed disdainfully. "I'm not surprised. Just his cup of tea, plan or no plan! He's just a twister at heart!"

Their conversation was interrupted by the arrival of their meal trays, brought from some mysterious source around a bend in the corridor by James V. King. He set them on the floor until he could unlock the doors and deliver them to the tables in the small cells, but at no time did he allow his watchful eyes to waver for one instant from his prisoners. It made for a dangerous journey as far as the soup was concerned, but the salad, joint and trifle made it without trouble. Simpson, peering in as his friends sat down to their meal, seemed surprised at the fare. Carruthers saw the look on his face and properly interpreted it.

"No," he said gently. "No vermin."

"So I see. I say," Simpson went on, turning to the suspicious warder who had retired to his stool and was keeping a sharp eye on the tall thin man to make sure he didn't surreptitiously take a bottle of acid from his pocket and attack the bars, "I don't suppose you could manage to arrange another tray—?"

To his complete amazement, King, James V. rose to his feet with alacrity and started off down the corridor, but his surprise turned to disappointment when he saw the action had not been occasioned by any desire to furnish Simpson with nourishment; it had been prompted by the approach of Sir Percival Pugh. The master-at-arms put the requisite distance between himself and the cells and then settled down on his heels, taking his usual broom straw from one of his many pockets and applying it to his teeth. The famous barrister came up, smiled first at Simpson who was the nearest and then treated the two imprisoned men to equal time as far as his smile was concerned.

Carruthers put down his knife and fork, but Briggs continued to sustain himself, keeping a watchful eye on their visitor as he did so. Sir Percival nodded to him pleasantly and seated himself on the small stool.

"Bon appétit."

Briggs made no acknowledgement of this politeness, continuing to chew on his joint. Carruthers studied Sir Percival's face.

"Any luck?"

Sir Percival nodded. "Quite a bit, actually. Sixty-four pounds, eight shillings, fourpence. Really not bad, considering the smallness of the stakes. Half of which sum," he continued, turning to Simpson, "is, technically, I suppose, yours. Although, under the circumstances, I hardly think—"

"No, no!" Carruthers said impatiently. "I mean any luck in determining which of the men you played with might have killed the Carpenters? That was the idea of the game, wasn't it?"

"Yes, it was," Sir Percival admitted, "but I'm afraid that part was a bit of a washout." He shook his head. "An amazingly complacent group. I did everything but reach across the table and help myself to their chips, and not a peep out of any of them."

Simpson was properly astounded. "Not even that huge chap with the ugly mug?"

Carruthers looked from one to the other. "Who?"

"A chap," Sir Percival explained, "named—believe it or not—Marmaduke Montmorency. As Clifford correctly states, large and unpretty. He offered his name to me more as a challenge, I do believe, than for any other purpose. He seemed to calm down considerably, however, when he heard mine. In fact, I believe I noted a touch of sympathy in his attitude from then on."

143

"He looked the sort who would stuff a chap through a port-hole just for the laughs," Simpson said. "Do you mean he allowed you to cheat him openly and said nothing?"

"That is precisely what I mean. Oh, he frowned once or twice, but that could have been headache. Mr. Montmorency really isn't a bad chap, you know. Large in the shoulders, but small in the brainpan, I'm afraid. I'm not even sure he knew he was being cheated. Wilkins, now—"

"Who?" Simpson frowned.

"The one who brayed whenever you said anything. His attitude with me was more chiding than anything else. He runs a small bookmaking establishment in the near East End and his outlook seemed to be that if he attempted my tactics with his customers, he'd be out of business in a week. Possibly," Sir Percival added, "with a broken back."

"What about the others?"

Sir Percival's broad brow wrinkled in concentration.

"There was a certain Arthur Tompkins, the one on my left. The one with the bifocal glasses," he added for the benefit of Simpson's recollection. "A certified accountant, by profession. I recall we split one hand—equal flushes, not a particularly simple thing to arrange. At any rate, I elected myself to divide the money in the pot. I took two shillings for each one I slid across the table to him. And still not the slightest argument."

"But why?" Carruthers demanded.

Sir Percival shrugged. "Possibly the man is weak in mathematics. . . ."

Simpson wasn't through with his catechism. "And that chap on your right?"

"A certain James Wellington. What he does in private life I do not know; but if he does not conduct his affairs with more acumen than he exhibited during that poker game, he'll never be a client of mine. He won't be able to afford it."

"But why?" Carruthers repeated, a touch of desperation in

his voice. "Why? Why would any one of them, let alone all of them, let you get away with it? Without one of them saying a word?"

"I can think of several reasons," Sir Percival said seriously, and then allowed his seriousness to dissolve into a soft smile, "none of which I am prepared at this moment to divulge."

"Great!" It was Briggs, entering the conversation the way he entered a room, bursting in with disgust. He had finished his trifle, cleaned his plates with his tongue and reseated them and was now girded for battle, energy from the joint flowing through his veins. "So all that came out of that fancy plan was that you picked yourself up thirty-odd pounds. Because regardless of how you feel about it, half of that money belongs to Cliff!"

"If you insist," Sir Percival said equably. "Actually, as you know, the cards were supposed to be recognizably marked, easing our task, and they were not. And my idea was to stake Clifford out as a sort of sacrificial goat, and again I was forced to take his place. However, I must admit the role seems to have ended up on the cutting-room floor, so I shall not argue the point."

"And what are your plans now?" Carruthers asked anxiously. "We're still in here and the murderer is still outside someplace. What's your next scheme? Scheme number one seems to have failed dismally."

"Scheme number two," Sir Percival reminded him. There was a touch of rebuke in his voice. "My scheme number one entailed saddling any one of a number of people with the crime or crimes and later, once we are all back home in England, defend him and get him off. I still like it, you know," he added gently.

"Defend him at our expense!" Briggs muttered.

His words were louder than he intended, or possibly he meant them to be heard. In any event, they were.

"Of course at your expense," Sir Percival said, amazed. "The man would be innocent, and his arrest and trial would merely be for your convenience." His tone indicated that anyone who thought he paid for defending innocent people out of his own pocket had to be crazy. He turned to Carruthers. "I don't suppose you've changed your mind on that score?"

"I certainly have not!" Carruthers shook his white locks indignantly. "Accuse an innocent man? Never!" His air of indignation faded; he peered through the bars at the famous barrister. "So what will you do now?"

There were several moments of silence while Sir Percival pondered. Then he shrugged delicately.

"We land tomorrow at Gibraltar," he said slowly. "The—"

"Gibraltar? So soon? I hadn't noticed!" Simpson beamed. "I recall, back in '15—" His voice trailed away apologetically in view of the look Sir Percival was bending upon him.

"As I was saying, we'll be there twenty-four hours. In that time our murderer can calmly visit the rock together with any other camera-laden peripatetic passenger and simply fail to return aboard. All of Spain is at his disposal, as well as the rest of Europe beyond. Not to mention Africa in the foreground . . ."

"From whence he can reach Asia Minor, and from there China, Japan or New Guinea," Briggs muttered sarcastically.

"Exactly," Sir Percival said agreeably and came to his feet.

"But why should the man?" Simpson asked, perplexed. "His failure to return to the ship will automatically cast suspicion on him, even if it doesn't brand him as the killer outright?"

"Of course we'd be freed if the foolish bloke breaks for it," Briggs said thoughtfully.

Carruthers snorted. "On what basis? Do you expect him to leave a note behind confessing all? All it would mean is that the murderer would be gone and we'd be even deeper in the soup." He turned back to Sir Percival. "You wouldn't be above paying someone not to get back on the ship, would you?"

Sir Percival smiled. "I wouldn't be above it—if someone else paid for it—but in this case, as you so intelligently point out, it would scarcely aid our case. No, if the murderer takes to his heels—as I expect he may well try to, unless stopped, he will do so without my connivance."

"But, to return to my first point, why would he run?" Carruthers demanded. "Nobody knows who he is, or even suspects him!"

"Ah!" said Sir Percival with an enigmatic smile and prepared to take his leave. He paused significantly a moment. "But suppose someone does suspect him? What then? Suppose someone does know him? Eh?"

He tapped the side of his patrician nose with a thin patrician finger, winked through the bars at the portly prisoner for good measure and ambled slowly down the corridor, pausing only long enough to exchange a word with James V. King. He turned for a final wave of encouragement and then was gone.

"Boobly squinch, that's what he knows!" Briggs said sourly.

Both Carruthers and Simpson were forced to suspect that Briggs was probably right. Sir Percival had put on a good show for their benefit, but it had been meant, they were sure, to raise their spirits and that was all. The plain truth was, in all likelihood, that in reality it all amounted to boobly squinch.

To Sir Percival, who had endured the hard gaze and harsher words of the toughest judges on the bench, the disapproving glare from his old friend Captain Manley-Norville glanced off with about as much effect as a raindrop on granite. The two men were seated comfortably in the Captain's suite adjoining the bridge; sunlight streamed through the windows which served the luxurious quarters in place of portholes, and the normally rolling waters off the mouth of the Tagus were as smooth as glass.

Sir Percival sipped a private brand of brandy far superior, he was sure, to that served in the bar, and looked at his companion with faint disapprobation. Attack, he knew from long

147

experience, was by far the best defense, and now that the social amenities had been observed in the traditional offering of alcoholic beverage, he knew the Captain was about to launch into a diatribe. Sir Percival meant to beat him to the punch.

"Really, Charles," he said, his voice fraught with reproach, "I do consider your conduct a bit reprehensible. You shouldn't have done it. You really shouldn't."

There was a moment's silence while the Captain choked on his drink. When at last he caught his breath he came close to exploding.

"*You* consider my conduct reprehensible? You consider *my* conduct reprehensible? You consider—" For a moment Captain Manley-Norville found himself at a loss for words, a rare occurrence. He set his glass aside and leaned forward, his square jaw thrust ahead like the prow of the S.S. *Sunderland*. "Now, you listen to me, Percy, my lad! Five minutes after that ridiculous bridge game between those two reprobates and the Carpenters —for whom I'm holding no wake—I was having words with the library steward. Burmese solitaire! The only reason I didn't have every deck of cards on board this ship commandeered and thrown overboard is that only those three were involved, and the other passengers were unaware of the markings. And I gave word to the steward that if either the Carpenters or any of those three ever got into a card game again, he was to hand them one of my personal decks I keep in case I have guests in for cards in my quarters." The Captain shook his head in disgust. "Burmese solitaire! Indeed!"

"A fine game," Sir Percival said, and sighed. "Unfortunately, it appears that too many people on board know the rules."

"A fine game! You *would* think so," said Captain Manley-Norville unkindly, and snorted. "And then, when Mr. Last-of-the-Mohicans Simpson comes walking into the card room, by whom is he accompanied? By none other than Sir Percival Pugh, no mean card player himself, and advocate for Mr. Simpson's imprisoned friends!"

"You do have your sources," Sir Percival murmured admiringly. "How did you ever hear of it so quickly?"

Captain Manley-Norville looked grim.

"You seem to forget that I am master of this ship," he said in a hard tone of voice. "And the library steward is under my command. He serves passengers, but he obeys me!"

"But even so, I fail to see—"

"Allow me to finish! When, as I said, Mr. Simpson comes walking in, he walks in with Sir Percival Pugh, who has the nerve to sit across from me at this moment, completely forgetting the many times I've sat in his drawing room of an evening and watched him entertain a roomful of guests with card tricks!"

Sir Percival felt it was time to get his oar in. He had purposely allowed the Captain to blow off steam, well aware that the other would be the weaker for it. He made his voice professionally cold.

"Still, Charles," he said, "in view of our years of friendship, I still consider your conduct reprehensible. When did you arrange it? When I went to wash my hands? Or am I correct in assuming your library steward arranged it at that time? And, more important, why did you do it?"

"Do what?" Captain Charles Everton Manley-Norville attempted to maintain his belligerent tone, but it was a failure. As Sir Percival had calculated, his previous explosion had taken a lot of wind from his sails, and besides, the chilly eye he was facing had made many a hardened prosecuting barrister quail in the past.

"You know very well what I mean!" Sir Percival's voice was scathing. "You—or your sycophant steward—told those players in that poker game some story that permitted them to lose to me without a murmur, even though I was obviously cheating them left and right. What was it you told them?" He dropped his voice calculatingly; it sounded all the more deadly for being merely conversational in tone. "Eh? What was it you told them? That I was gathering material for a book? That I was practicing for a stage turn at card tricks?"

"I—"

"Or did you say I was doing a thesis on toleration to cheating and merely wished their reactions?"

"I—"

"Or did you simply tell them I was scatty? A kleptomaniac at the card table, so to speak? And that their losses would be returned to them by my keeper after the game if they would only humor me? That one is my choice."

Captain Manley-Norville felt he had to defend himself.

"Percy, the fact is that there has been too much cheating on this ship as it is. The fact is that you were cheating passengers, as well; and it's my duty to protect them. As I said before, you seem to forget that I am master of this ship. And you also seem to forget that the master of a ship has certain responsibilities!"

Sir Percival shook his head in pity at the weakness of the argument.

"And you seem to forget, Charles, that there is a murderer loose on your ship! And the only one you are protecting with your interference in my affairs is him!" He leaned forward. "Do you honestly believe that I was cheating those men for the thruppeny–ha'penny winnings involved?"

"Well, no, but—"

"Well, no, but what? The fact is you didn't think at all, and that's the fact! Somebody killed Mrs. Carpenter, and you seem to have completely forgotten it, and that's the fact!"

"Briggs was right there in the room," Captain Manley-Norville said darkly. He seemed to imply that if Briggs was guilty, then his—the Captain's—actions regarding the poker game would somehow be defensible.

"Don't try to make up for your past errors by multiplying them," Sir Percival advised coldly. "Among the many other points I could prove—to free Briggs if I wished to—is that you know as well as I do that had Mrs. Carpenter ever faced Briggs with him holding a knife, the chances are she would have made him eat it. He didn't come up to her shoulders, and she probably outweighed him a good four stone."

"Unless he crept up on her and stabbed her in the back."

"How do you creep up on somebody in a bathroom roughly three feet square?" Sir Percival asked curiously. "Not to mention that Mrs. Carpenter was stabbed from the front. Besides, Briggs hasn't the temperament for a stabbing." He thought awhile, remembering the Murder League, and changed his tone a bit. "Anyway, not a woman. And certainly not for free." He shook his head a bit forlornly. "I was attempting to discover, in that poker game, who the Carpenters had cheated to the extent of engendering resentment to the extent of murder. I had hoped that one or more of the players would demonstrate equal resentment in my case, and—to coin a cliché—unmask himself." His eyes came up, cold again. "You put an end to that quickly enough."

"I'm sorry, Percy," said the Captain contritely.

"You should be. I will admit," Sir Percival said, thinking back, "that for a few minutes there, when my cheating didn't bring out the faintest snarl or the slightest resentment, I considered seriously the possibility that the four of them might have worked as a team to handle the Carpenters. I thought they might even have utilized the services of their wives and/or girl friends. Looking at that group playing canasta in the other corner and listening to them, I could conceive of no crime they might not be capable of committing. And, of course, all of them had been victimized at one time or another by the Carpenters at the bridge table. But then I thought that four murderers—or eight, adding wives and/or girl friends—was a bit much, so I looked elsewhere for an explanation of their complaisance at being cheated. And, of course, lit upon you first out of the box.”

“I can only repeat that I’m sorry.”

“Water over the dam,” said Sir Percival philosophically and changed the subject. “What’s on the docket in the form of entertainment tonight? The ship’s newspaper hasn’t been too informative, lately.”

“The master-at-arms is also our reporter. He’s been busy, you know.”

“If picking your teeth with a broom straw constitutes business, he’s been busy,” Sir Percival admitted. “You haven’t answered my question. How do the peasants frolic this eve?”

“Captain’s party, as a matter of fact.” Captain Manley-Norville unconsciously preened a bit as he said it. “Formal, you know.”

“Well, I wouldn’t worry about that. Easy enough to cancel. And what time do we dock tomorrow?”

“Elevenish in the morning. But about the party tonight—”

“One of those things. One can’t have everything. The party, I’m afraid, is out.”

“But, why?” Captain Manley-Norville almost wailed.

“Because, Charles, pet, tomorrow, as you say, we dock at eleven. And our murderer may well decide not to take a chance by returning to the ship. While he may feel safe at the moment —or may not—he knows, as well as I do, that little Timmy Briggs is as pure as the driven snow, at least as far as killing Mrs. Carpenter is concerned. And eventually, of course, this fact is bound to come to light, despite the distractions placed in the paths of justice by ship’s masters. At that time, of course, suspicious glances are going to be cast in other directions. One of them might well be his. Our next stop after Gibraltar is Funchal, I believe, on an island from which it is relatively difficult for a fugitive to escape. If I were an enterprising murderer not wishing to take chances, I do think I would leave the ship at Gibraltar tomorrow and not return.”

"But what's that got to do with my party tonight?"

"Tonight, Charles, we shall turn our efforts to more vital purposes." He came to his feet, smiling faintly. "In any event, Captains' parties are old hat. Tonight we shall give the passengers of the S.S. *Sunderland* entertainment in a more unusual form."

Despite the loss of his party, Captain Manley-Norville found himself intrigued.

"In what form?" he asked.

"In the form of a Coroner's Inquest," Sir Percival said quietly, and moved toward the door.

12

When Miss Carol Grumkin of Golder's Green first went to work for the accounting firm of Tompkins and Struthers as secretary to its president, Mr. Arthur Tompkins, she had hoped—as all young people starting out on their careers should do—quite naturally for rapid promotion and quick success; nor was she unwilling to work for them. The efficacy of this philosophy could not have been better demonstrated, for now, less than six months later, her services had become so indispensable that Mr. Tompkins had brought her along on the cruise of the S.S. *Sunderland,* installing her in an adjoining cabin, in order to handle any correspondence that might reach them en route as well as any other secretarial duties that might arise of a general business nature.

It was therefore difficult for Mr. Tompkins to refuse when the Captain of the *Sunderland*—wishing to keep some record of the proceedings of his first shipboard Coroner's Inquest and having no other substitute—requested the services of Miss Grumkin to take down a shorthand account of the action, for insertion in the ship's log. Mr. Tompkins attempted to explain to Miss

Grumkin in the privacy of their joint staterooms that her talents in that direction were really not the equal of a standard courtroom stenotypist's, but Miss Grumkin, offered a share of the limelight, was not about to refuse. After all, when Arty-Barty was a guest for dinner at the Captain's table one evening, she had been forced to settle for a salad in her stateroom, and when Smarty-Arty wanted to play bridge or poker all day instead of paying attention to her, she wasn't even permitted to don her bikini—which she set off to spectacular advantage—and sit around the pool with its handsome lifeguard. Given such conditions, Mr. Lardy-Arty could scarcely expect his normal authority to prevail.

This history, therefore, depends a bit for its accuracy on Miss Carol Grumkin's notes, and while there may be an occasional hiatus where a witness used more than a two-syllable word, in general they are not as bad as might be expected. For one thing —despite her appearance in a bikini—Miss Grumkin had actually taken a three-month course in stenography and had even passed, although her fellow students credited this miracle to reasons other than scholastic ability. This, however, could well have been mere jealousy. A better reason for the relative accuracy of this report, it is to be judged, is that Sir Percival Pugh was kind enough to edit it for the sake of the Captain's record, adding little things like punctuation, correcting spelling and even being so thoughtful as to put in local dialect when used to enhance the dramatic quality of his masterful interrogation. There are some who may feel he used the occasion to build up his brilliance in the case, paying little attention to Miss Grumkin's actual notes, but again, this may be mere jealousy. Suffice to say, what we have here is what now reposes as An Addition to the Log of the S.S. *Sunderland,* as well as in the archives of the New Scotland Yard. . . .

Timothy Briggs tramped morosely up the carpeted stairway

from E Deck to the Promenade Deck and the Main Salon where the inquest was to be held, grumbling all the way. At his side Billy-boy Carruthers trudged, silent and thoughtful. Before them the same husky sailor who had assisted at their arrest marched evenly, while King, James V. brought up the rear, sorry he had not been permitted to handcuff his prisoners and even sadder that the Captain had turned down his request for a submachine gun, a shotgun—or even a .22-caliber pistol—to make sure they did not escape. James V. King was determined that his charges would be delivered in one piece and would not disappear in a puff of puce smoke—a thing he had seen accomplished on the stage of the Palladium once—or at least not if he could prevent it.

"Inquest!" Briggs muttered in deep disgust. "All it means is being paraded in front of a bunch of gaping idiots, like the crowds watching the Christians in a Roman arena. What does old Pugh think he's going to prove by all this nonsense?"

"He probably thinks he can get us out of the soup this way," Carruthers suggested evenly. He looked sideways. "Do you have any major objections? Or would you really prefer to spend the rest of the cruise in the brig?"

"Might just as well, the tight rein you keep on our having any fun," Briggs said sourly. He grimaced as if in pain. "And all because of some idiot writer a million miles away!" He looked up at the calm blue eyes of his rotund companion. "I say, Billy-boy—if by some miracle old Pugh does manage to pull it off and they strike the shackles and all that, how about giving the old S.S. *Sunderland* and her crew the back of our necks at Gibraltar and flying back home? Eh? I've about had the bloody bounding main!"

Carruthers glanced down at the wizened face staring up at him so earnestly. He smiled faintly. "Beginning to think that possibly Sir Percival can pull it off, eh?"

"Oh, he can twist a jury in a courtroom around his little

finger, I don't deny that," Briggs admitted grudgingly, "but he isn't in a courtroom here. I wouldn't go so far as to say he'll pull any rabbits out of his hat as far as the Captain of this tub is concerned. Let's just say that while I don't necessarily have a lot of faith, I still have a bit of hope."

"A touch of charity wouldn't be amiss, either," Carruthers commented dryly, and continued his march up the stairs.

" 'Ere now!" said James V. King, sternly. He raised his arms, simulating possession of a weapon. "That'll be enough o' that chatter, see? Yer prisoners, and don't yer forget it!"

The library steward, faced with the problem at short notice of converting the Main Salon into a courtroom scene suitable for a Coroner's Inquest, didn't boggle for a moment. Fifteen years of arranging for masquerade parties in which the Salon took on the appearance of everything from the Casbah, to Carnival in Rio, to Waikiki, to the poop deck of a Spanish galleon, had given him much valuable practice. And as an avid cinema fan in his rare free time, he had witnessed many a vis-à-vis between prosecuting counsel and defense advocate before a gavel-pounding bewigged judge, so the scene was clearly fixed in his mind. His only problem was that he couldn't rightly recall whether a Coroner's Inquest took place in a court of law or a morgue. Fortunately he opted for the courtroom, and he had done himself proud.

The relatively low ceiling of the Main Salon, unfortunately, was not constructed to accommodate the multiplicity of levels favored by English justice since the days of King John and Magna Carta. Still, the steward had not done badly. The bandstand would serve excellently for the Captain acting the part of the chief officer of the inquest, and it was still large enough to accommodate a small table for Miss Grumkin, an added attraction from any point of view. The prisoners, while unable to be placed exactly midway in height between the bench and the gallery, were still able to be differentiated in elevation by having their chairs put atop one of the enormous coffee tables that dotted the area. A third level might have been developed from the counter top of the main bar, but Sir Percival had ruled this out himself. He didn't mind spectators leaving the proceedings to locate alcoholic sustenance elsewhere, but he wanted his witnesses and potential suspects within sight. The main bar, therefore, remained open and—incidentally—did a land-office business in the next few hours.

Captain Charles Everton Manley-Norville, resplendent in the white uniform he had intended for the evening in any event, and with his chest draped with the plethora of medals he had accumulated honorably during the war, surveyed the crowd from his vantage point. He had to admit that Percy Pugh had a good point in putting on an inquest for entertainment rather than the usual Captain's Party, and for a moment he wondered if it might not be a good idea to incorporate it in the ship's general program for passenger divertissement. It would mean, of course, that the band would be idle—and therefore paid for not working—and the Captain dropped the thought at once. It struck him the band did little enough as it was, especially since not a one of them was familiar with anything more recent than the schottische. He put the idea behind him and resumed studying the passengers crowding into the room.

The witnesses requested by Sir Percival had been advised of their special status and were seated in a row along the edge of the dance floor, which was now the main arena for the pyrotechnics planned by the famous advocate for the evening. All of the witnesses appeared guilty of something or other, if only for their selection. The balance of the seats in the huge room were rapidly filling up, and waiters were quietly moving from spot to spot filling the orders of the thirsty. Miss Grumkin, well supplied with notebooks and sharpened pencils, was busily practicing pothooks and hoping none of the witnesses were tongue-tied, or spoke American, or anything like that.

Captain Manley-Norville consulted his wristwatch and leaned over, tapping Sir Percival Pugh on the shoulder.

"I say, Percy," he said in a low voice, "how do you start one of these things going?"

"You simply start them," Sir Percival replied. His eyes passed the Captain to rest on the expanse of thigh uncovered by Miss Grumkin's miniskirt; he cleared his throat and forcibly returned his eyes front and center. "Clap your hands, or stamp your foot or something. Haven't you ever quelled a mutiny? And, by the way, you'd best call me Sir Percival when you address me in front of the audience, so to speak. If you don't mind."

"Right-O, Percy," said the Captain agreeably. He straightened up, surveyed the mob a moment and then slammed his fist onto the leader's music stand, hurting himself considerably. He promised to himself that the band leader would unlearn sixteen schottisches before the next trip and cleared his throat. "If I might have your attention," he began, nursing his wounded hand in the clenched palm of his other. "If I might just have your attention, please. . . ."

There was the usual last-minute frantic shuffling in the room; those whose throats had been as balm in Gilead a moment before now found the sudden tickle imperative, and coughed. Captain Manley-Norville waited patiently until the normal unrest had quieted itself and then spoke again. This time his years of authority asserted themselves clearly. He made no move to rise from his chair; if anything he seemed to settle himself in it even more firmly.

"This is a Coroner's Inquest," he said in a quiet voice that nonetheless carried through the huge room. The last vestiges of the shuffling instantly ceased. His cold eye swept his charges. "It will be conducted in the main by Sir Percival Pugh, the well-known barrister, although I do not promise not to interrupt the proceedings as I see fit. Sir Percival is, by pure chance, a passenger on this ship, as are all the others involved in the tragedy we are here investigating."

He reached out, sipped at a glass that appeared to contain water but did not, and returned to his theme. His audience had not moved an inch during the interlude.

"The purpose of this inquest is to determine, as best may be determined, the facts concerning the recent unfortunate demise of another passenger, Mrs. Mazie Carpenter, and the mysterious disappearance—in which, I might mention, foul play, with cause, is suspected—of her husband, Mr. Maxwell Carpenter. . . ."

Even the waiters had frozen in their tracks The bartender, attempting to shake a cocktail silently, desisted. All eyes were on the white-uniformed figure speaking so dryly from the platform.

"I mean," said Captain Manley-Norville, unapologetically, "foul play is suspected, with cause. Not quite the same thing." His glance dared anyone to argue with his syntax; nobody did. Satisfied, he continued. "Certain facts are known; I shall mention only the most important and leave it to Sir Percival in his interrogation of the witnesses to bring the balance out for the record. The main fact under consideration is that two days ago Mrs. Carpenter was found in the bath of her stateroom murdered: stabbed to death. A Mr. Briggs is held for the murder and has been housed in the ship's detention brig. Sir Percival, in addition to conducting this inquest, is also the advocate for Mr. Briggs as well as for Mr. Carruthers, whom the late Mrs. Carpenter accused of attempted assault upon her person, and who has also been under restraint. . . ."

Sir Percival could not but respect the language of the Captain. He suspected—quite correctly—that the chief officer of the S.S. *Sunderland* had spent the afternoon boning up on barratry and assorted crimes at sea. He rocked back on his heels and waited while the pontifical voice continued.

"These are the only facts I shall state, for they are not only provable but a matter of record. All other matters of record, from this point on, I shall leave to Sir Percival. May I mention but one thing more"—his cold eye swept the mob to silence, utter silence—"and that is this: it is not incumbent upon this court to arrive at any conclusion. We have no coroner's jury, or jury of any sort; nor is any required in circumstances of this nature. We are at sea in international waters. Any pertinent information brought out in the course of this inquiry will be transmitted to the British authorities in Gibraltar tomorrow. Nonetheless"—his voice sharpened perceptibly as did the attention of his rapt audience—"it would be a vast mistake on the part of anyone called upon to give testimony before this inquest to assume that truthful statements are not essential, nor that this court carries no authority. This ship is British territory, and I am master of this ship. And as master of a ship in international waters, I am the supreme authority. Do not forget this fact. I can—and will—punish any false statement or evasion as I see fit." His cold eye swept the crowd. "I wish that point to be eminently clear."

There was dead silence for several seconds, and then those who had been holding back allowed their coughs and sneezes temporary freedom. Captain Manley-Norville took advantage of the lull to swing about in his chair, speaking to the wide-eyed girl behind him.

"Miss Grumkin—did you get all that?"

"All what? Oh!" She stared at him in alarm. "Was that all part of it? Was I supposed to be taking all that down? I'm sorry. I didn't know. You didn't say anything about when to start. . . ."

Witness Arthur Tompkins, third from the left in the witness row, looked at the ceiling for comfort and then brought his eyes down and covered them with his hand. He wondered, not for the first time, if possibly Mrs. Tompkins might not have been a better companion for this particular trip, and—also not for the first time—rejected the thought as being patently ridiculous.

"Well," said the Captain in a vain attempt to sound understanding, "I'd suggest we try and pick it up from here on out, eh?"

He tried desperately to smile and turned back to the audience, wiping away the grimace instantly. Behind him a pencil scratched with tortoise speed across a notebook page; the corner of a pink tongue protruded from richly painted lips and was clamped upon by pearly teeth in a spasm of concentration. Captain Manley-Norville leaned back in his chair and spoke in a heavy voice, announcing the start of proceedings.

"Sir Percival Pugh!"

Sir Percival rose from the chair he had taken and placed beneath the bandstand, moving forward a step, studying the audience, bringing them under his magnetic charm. In matters of this nature, he was in his element, a master of handling the emotions and thoughts of those who fell under the spell of his rich voice.

"Ladies and gentlemen, fellow passengers. Murder has been committed, murder most foul, murder crying for justice, for revenge. And a man is in custody for that murder, a murder he did not commit. And another man is in custody charged with an assault he did not commit. These are simple facts to prove and I shall do so in a few moments. I—"

There seemed to be a minor sensation in the back of the room, and for a moment Sir Percival wondered what he had said to cause it, but it turned out that someone had merely popped a contact lens, and the matter was quickly resolved when someone else stepped on it with a crunch. Order was restored in seconds, and the eminent barrister resumed his statement.

"As I was saying, I shall, in a very few moments, prove the innocence of my clients. But more important than freeing these men—which is a minor task—is to use this inquest if possible to uncover the true villain, the person who did commit this murder. That is the true purpose of an inquiry of this nature, and to this end—"

He paused at the slight tap on his shoulder and turned politely. Captain Manley-Norville was bending as low as he could in his chair, assuming a position indicating clearly he wished privacy for his words. Sir Percival moved his ear until it was practically touching the other's lips. His own barely moved.

"Yes?"

"I say, Percy," the Captain whispered, "let's keep it all within reason, shall we? I mean, after all! Saying you can prove this Briggs chap innocent in a matter of minutes! Really!"

"But, my dear Charles, I can. I could have anytime since you put him into that cell."

"Then why the devil didn't you do so?"

Sir Percival swung about and stared at his old friend in surprise. "And have him loosed upon this ship any sooner than absolutely necessary? Is that what you really would have preferred?"

"Oh, ah!" the Captain whispered in understanding.

"But with Gibraltar coming up tomorrow, I had no choice. Now, if you don't mind, I'll get on with it."

"Of course," said the Captain apologetically and sank back into his chair again.

To the audience it appeared as if the two had been discussing a technical matter; Miss Grumkin may also have thought so, but she did not raise the question as to whether the whispered conversation should be included in the record, mainly because she had just finished putting down the symbols for "Ladies and Gentlemen" and was trying desperately to remember what had followed. Oh, well, she thought philosophically, Smarty-Arty has a fabulous memory—he'll tell me later what everyone said. He'd better!

163

Sir Percival returned to his task, pausing only long enough to sip at a glass that appeared to contain water—and actually did. He patted his lips and turned to his audience once again. Dead silence fell as soon as he began to speak.

"We return once again, ladies and gentlemen, to our central theme: the purpose of an inquest is to arrive at the truth, or as much of the truth as can be arrived at, regarding the death of the victim, in this case, Mrs. Mazie Carpenter. To this end I shall interrogate witnesses and see what can be learned. But before we can get down to that, let us handle this matter of my clients and clear the board—or, more appropriately in the circumstances, the decks—for the more important phases of this investigation.

"First, then, let us take up the matter of Mr. Carruthers and his so-called sexual-assault attempt against the person of Mrs. Carpenter."

He turned to face the accused seated on top of the coffee table. His audience followed his gaze as if hypnotized and then returned their eyes to his face as he took up where he had left off.

"To begin with, ladies and gentlemen, let me say that there is no legal basis for holding my client. Mrs. Carpenter is no longer with us to press charges if she wished to, and she passed on before she made any written, formal charge against my client; again, even if she had wished to. . . ."

He paused as a buzz swept the room. Briggs leaned over, whispering to Carruthers.

"That twister! If that's true, why didn't he say so days ago? And gotten you free?"

"To keep me out of trouble, I suspect," Carruthers said with narrowed eyes, and returned his attention to his defense.

"I might also mention," Sir Percival continued evenly, "that it also would have been the easiest thing in the world for my client to have claimed that his age—for he is no longer in the flush of youth—made it impossible for him to have attempted such an attack, or at least to have attempted it with any reasonable hope of assured success. But again, you will note we do not choose to use this defense, either. . . ."

From the corner of his eye he saw the look of wonder combined with relief that covered Billy-boy Carruthers' rubicund face. Sir Percival grinned inwardly and continued, his face outwardly revealing nothing but his sincere desire to seek out and expose the truth.

"The fact is that Mrs. Carpenter was sexually attractive, and Mr. Carruthers, male to the core, was well aware of it. To Mr. Carruthers, all women are attractive. The truth is that Mr. Carruthers is possibly more to be pitied than censured, being, if anything, oversexed. He finds women attractive and—although some men might find this hard to credit—most beautiful women find Mr. Carruthers equally attractive. And this has nothing to do with the fact that, as one of the co-winners of the Jarvis award this year, he came into a veritable fortune. No, it is that inner chemical so hard to explain. . . ."

He paused while the buzz returned, louder this time. He noted all eyes turned momentarily to study Carruthers, and he was far from surprised to note that the women in the room were looking at the rotund man speculatively, and a few of them were even unconsciously beginning to nod their heads. Psychology, it's wonderful, Pugh thought, containing the twinkle in his eye, and waited patiently. Carruthers was now looking at him with a frown of speculation; Briggs with even more than his usual suspicion. Simpson, in the front row of spectators, was wondering how—during all these years—he had failed to note the mutual attraction between Billy-boy and members of the opposite sex.

Sir Percival's face remained calm, almost majestic, but his inward chortling increased as he pictured Billy-boy Carruthers faced with a mob of adoring women. And if that doesn't get those three to leave the boat tomorrow and catch a plane home, he thought to himself gleefully, then nothing will! Which should give me a bit of peace and quiet for the rest of the trip and should also be worth all the free champagne from Charles that I can drink until I get home!

The chatter in the room began to subside. Sir Percival allowed it to die a natural death before he took command again.

"But, then—-one might say—if women find Mr. Carruthers so irresistible, apparently Mrs. Mazie Carpenter was not one of them, or else why would she have shrieked for help? Well, as any doctor can tell you, there are women like that—women who enjoy being pursued—and apparently Mrs. Carpenter was one of them. It is all too obvious, as one studies the psychology and the facts, that Mrs. Carpenter's screams were merely a further means on her part of indicating how much Mr. Carruthers' attentions really meant to her."

He turned a harsh look upon James V. King, sitting among the witnesses.

"If anyone deserves censure in this matter," he said, his voice accusing, "I suggest it be the master-at-arms, who, by breaking into that stateroom at that particular moment, interrupted who knows what lovely idyll?"

He stepped back, indicating his statement was over. There was a burst of applause, instantly quelled as Captain Manley-Norville rapped sharply on the music stand with his left hand.

"I think," he said in his deep voice, "that we all owe Sir Percival a vote of thanks for bringing the truth into the open. I also think we owe Mr. Carruthers an apology for falsely detaining him. He may step down."

The Captain's eyes searched out the master-at-arms; the look he gave the man clearly indicated what he, the Captain, thought of people who recklessly destroyed ship's property which he, the Captain, would have to account for later to the line's directors. Behind him Miss Grumkin struggled bravely with her pothooks. It had occurred to her that possibly putting down every fifth word—or a reasonable facsimile—might handle the situation, assuming she could remember to fill in the blanks later.

Sir Percival nodded his head with appropriate gratitude for the court's decision and then stepped forward again. The buzzing in the room instantly stopped.

"Before we can get to the purpose of this inquest as stated earlier," he said, "there is still the matter of my client, Mr. Briggs. Again, I'm afraid, a matter easily cleared up. . . ."

He paused impressively for a few seconds and then referred to a piece of paper which seemed to have appeared in his hand by legerdemain. His eye passed over little Briggs, sitting pitifully alone on the coffee table, and came to rest on a person in the row of witnesses. His audience tensed a bit. Now they were dealing with a matter of murder! Sir Percival appreciated the change in emotional ambience and treated it with appropriate respect by dropping his voice so that every ear had to strain to hear.

"Mr. Alfred Williamson, if you please. . . ."

13

Interrogation conducted by Sir Percival Pugh:

Q: Your name is Alfred A. Williamson?

A: Yer called me name, didn't yer? An' I come, didn't I? Think I don't know me own name? 'Ow many Fred A. Williamsons yer think they got on this 'ere bucket?

Q: I don't know, but I'm beginning to suspect one too many. However: you are employed in the maintenance division of this ship?

A: Now yer got it, cock!

Captain Manley-Norville *(interrupting):* Now see here, my man! You'll watch your tongue when you're addressing Sir Percival, do you hear?

A: Oh raht, Capt'n. Yar, sir!

Sir Percival Pugh *(resumes):* To get back to where we were: on Wednesday, July 17—two days ago—you were sent by your section chief to B Deck, Stateroom B-67, for the purpose of repairing a broken door?

A: Who else was to fix it?

Q: I have no idea. Would you answer my question, please?

A: Oh raht. Sure, I was sent.

Q: Could you give us the details?

A: What details? Day before ol' fink King James the Vee, 'im an' a sailor bustit in the door and practically took 'er raht off the 'inges. Bent 'em somethin' fierce. It 'ad to be the sailor what done the job, becos ol' King James, 'e couldn't bust 'is way out of 'is pijamers without 'is ol' lady's 'elp.

Sir Percival (*addressing the Captain*): Never mind, Captain. I can handle this. Now, Mr. Williamson, how does it happen that the door was broken on Tuesday, and it was only on the Wednesday that you were sent to repair it?

A: Like I told you, them 'inges was all twisted-like. They 'ad to fashion up some new ones in the shop. An' them blacksmiths don't work like us fitters, if yer was to ask me!

Q: But was the door open, then, during the nearly twenty-four hours that the hinges were being fashioned?

A: Naw, sir. Them ol' 'inges was still on the door, only it meant yer 'ad to tug like a baskit to get the door open.

Q: I see. But what about the lock?

A: That was a proper mess, a dead loss. They rigged up a 'asp and a padlock-like. I took 'em orf when I fixed the new lock in place, like.

Q: I see. So that even though almost a day had passed since the accident to the door, access was still barred for unauthorized personnel. But tell me, how would the steward or stewardess be able to get in to clean the room?

A: Orl our padlocks got master keys, same as the door locks. Stewards, stewardesses, master-at-arms, Captain—they all got master keys. Otherwise it'd be a proper mess, sir, the way passengers lose keys! You wouldn't believe!

Q: I would believe. Now, to return to your fixing the door on Wednesday: at what time were you sent up there? Or, better, at what time did you complete your task?

A: They tol' me yer'd ask that question, so I brung me time card, like. Got to punch in an' punch out on every bleedin' job like a bleedin' convick! Anyways, it was eleven-oh-five I punched in, and the job took an hour on the button. See?

Q: I see, indeed. Now, as I understand it, you were finished with your work when you met Mr. Briggs in the corridor, is that correct?

A: You got it, cock! I mean, yar, sir!

Q: And you gave him the keys to the cabin, asking him if he would be so kind as to leave them at the purser's desk since—in your coveralls—you were not encouraged to go to the purser's square. Is that correct?

A: That's raht, and 'e was a real gent, 'e was, cos 'e said 'e'd do it. An' if yer tryin' to 'ang anythin' on a gent like 'im, orl I can say is I 'opes yer ain't expectin' no 'elp from me!

Q: My dear Mr. Williamson, I am Mr. Briggs' counsel. I am trying to free him of this ridiculous charge. Haven't you been paying any attention at all since you've been in this room?

A: I was lookin' around, see? I don't get up 'ere much except to fix somethin' broke, and then I got to get back to the shop quick-like, see? But if yer tryin' to 'elp the ol' man, I owes yer an apology, sir. I didn't understand. I'll answer any other questions yer got, any way yer wants 'em answered, if that'll 'elp, sir.

Q: I appreciate your kind intentions, Mr. Williamson, but the truth will do just fine. Tell me, would it have been possible for Mr. Briggs to have entered the cabin—B-67—during the period when you were working on the door? I mean, did you have to return to stores for tools or materials or things of that nature during the hour you were assigned to repair the door?

A: Not bloody likely! I mean, naw, sir. They tol' me what was wrong an' I brung the lot with me. Our chief, he screams if yer got to go back fer anythin'. A ship ain't like a bleedin' plumber's shop on land, and yer can believe it!

Q: I believe it. So Mr. Briggs could therefore only have

gained entrance to cabin B-67 after twelve-oh-five, according to your testimony. Only after you handed him the keys?

A: That's raht, sir.

Q: Thank you, Mr. Williamson. You're excused. You may return to your seat.

A: Raht, sir.

SIR PERCIVAL *(to the line of witnesses):* May I next have the ship's surgeon on the stand? Thank you. . . .

Q: Your name is Doctor Hugh Ramsey?

A: That is correct.

Q: On Wednesday, July 17—two days ago—you were called to the cabin of Mrs. Carpenter? Stateroom B-67?

A: I was.

Q: May I ask by whom? And at what hour?

A: The master-at-arms, Mr. James—I mean, Mr. King— called me on the cabin telephone telling me of the accident, and I took my bag and went there at once. The call came at about twelve-ten, I should judge, because I was just preparing to go to lunch, and I remember the second gong had just sounded. I was at the Carpenter stateroom within a matter of two or three minutes.

Q: And, may I ask, what did you find?

A: The stewardess was having hysterics; I told the master-at-arms to take her to hospital and have one of my nurses give her a sedative. I then entered the bath, where I had been told the accident had taken place. The body of Mrs. Carpenter was lying in the shower stall, folded up, but it was still evident that she had been stabbed several times in the chest and abdomen.

Q: What did you do then?

A: The first thing I did was to determine that death had, indeed, taken place, although there wasn't the faintest doubt. I checked for pulse and breath. There was none. Once it had been determined that she was beyond medical care, I returned to the stateroom proper and telephoned the Captain, informing him of the circumstances.

Q: And then?

A: I waited until the Captain arrived. He was followed almost immediately by Mr. James—I mean, King—who was returning from the infirmary. He had stopped in his quarters and brought along a camera and flashbulbs, and he took pictures of the corpse from several angles. When he had finished, I was permitted to have the body removed to hospital.

Q: Did you there perform an autopsy?

A: No. I felt the cause of death was sufficiently clear. And the master-at-arms, Mr. James—I mean, King—gave me to understand that the identity of the murderer was clear.

Q: But, still, you must have arrived at some idea of the time of death?

A: Well, I did take the body temperature and recorded it for the proper land authorities, and I also stated in my notes the condition of advancement of blood coagulation on the scene, although depending upon the type of shower the victim had taken, hot or cold, these times can vary greatly.

Q: I note you say "depending upon the type of shower the victim had taken." Was the body, then, wet?

A: No. It was completely dry.

Q: But then, either the shower had not been taken, or the water must have evaporated from the skin. Is this not true?

A: Yes, but it's not surprising. After all, after several hours—

Q: Did you say several hours?

A: Yes, why? Mrs. Carpenter had been dead a minimum of three or four hours when I saw her. However, the exact time—

Interruption by a minor sensation in the court—the Main Salon, that is. Captain Manley-Norville raps for order, now using a baton he has discovered on the music stand. When at last the furor dies down, he speaks.

Captain Manley-Norville: It seems eminently clear to me that it has been proven without a doubt that Mr. Briggs could not possibly have committed this crime, because of the time element involved. He is therefore permitted to stand down. His purpose in entering the stateroom in the first place will be overlooked in view of the fact that nothing seems to be missing from the premises, and also in view of the fact that he has already suffered two days of incarceration. However, in this case—as differentiated from that of Mr. Carruthers—I specifically wish the record to show that no apology is being offered him. Miss Grumkin? Have you gotten that?

Miss Grumkin *(close to tears and now writing in longhand, frantically):* . . . overlooked in view of the fact . . .

Captain Manley-Norville: Sir Percival, may I congratulate you on a brilliant exposition, one well up to the always-high standards you are so deservedly known for. And now, if we're all through—

Sir Percival Pugh: Captain Manley-Norville, if I might interrupt: we are far from finished with this inquest. In fact, we are just getting to it, if I may say so. I should like to continue to interrogate Dr. Ramsey, if I may.

Captain Manley-Norville *(sinking back in his seat):* Oh, yes, of course. But first, steward—if you'd bring me a bit more of this—ah—vichy? The bartender on duty knows the brand. . . .

Q: Now, doctor, to return a moment to the scene of the crime: was any weapon in evidence?

A: No; but from what Mr. James—I mean King—told me, he said the murderer was so covered with lipstick when he was seen that he could have been carrying a blood-stained dirk in his teeth and nobody would have noticed.

Q: I rather doubt that statement, and in any event it is scarcely relevant since Mr. Briggs has been proven innocent. As

173

for the master-at-arms, we'll get to his testimony soon enough, and I'd prefer it direct.

A: Yes, sir.

Q: To return to Stateroom B-67, you were in there not too many hours before the events you have just described, were you not?

A: I was. As a matter of fact, all three of us—myself, Captain Manley-Norville, and Mr. King—I mean, James—no, I mean, King, don't I?—were in there quite late the evening before. Midnightish, I should judge. Mrs. Carpenter had requested us to investigate the disappearance of her husband.

Q: I see. And what did you do? I mean, in what manner did you conduct this investigation?

A: Well, Mr.—the master-at-arms was sent to pick up a gang and search the ship, while the Captain and myself went over the bedroom and bath in some detail, in case there might have been any visible signs of foul play, you see.

Q: And did you discover any?

A: Well, we found some blood on the porthole sill that seemed to both of us to be rather significant. It looked very much as if someone might have put Mr. Carpenter through the porthole into the sea—I understand he had made enemies—and in trying to hold back, he might have cut himself on the edge of the hinge, which has a rather sharp edge. I cannot account for the blood being there, otherwise.

Q: Very interesting. Tell me, doctor, did you make any attempt to determine if the bloodstain on the porthole sill was of human origin, or of other animal origin?

A: Why, no. I had no reason to suspect it to be other than human blood. There are no animals allowed in the cabins.

Q: Do you have the necessary chemicals in your surgery to make such an analysis?

A: Oh, yes. Of course. There are various tests, but the simplest and quickest is merely to stain a dried preparation with

selected dyes and measure the diameter of the red blood cor-
puscles. The human red blood corpuscle is about 1/3200 of an
inch in diameter. A dog, now—

Q: I would rather not undertake a short course in forensics
at this time, if you do not mind. I suggest the blood on that
porthole sill is not human. Nor from a dog. I suggest it is
chicken blood.

A: *Chicken blood?*

Q: Yes. I'm sorry if I startled you. Would it be possible,
doctor, while I interrogate other witnesses, for you to do a rapid
check upon my hypothesis?

A: Of course.

Q: You are, therefore, excused, but I shall resume taking
your testimony immediately upon your return.

A: Thank you. I shall hurry.

SIR PERCIVAL *(turning once again to the witness bench):* I
suppose we'd do as well starting on the card players next. Let
me see . . . Mr. Montmorency? Your name is Marmaduke
Montmorency?

A: And your name is Percival Pugh.

Q: Yes. We are partners in suffering. Tell me, Mr. Montmorency, you were involved in a bridge game not too long ago
with the Carpenters, were you not?

A: I was.

Q: They cheated you, did they not?

A: They did.

Q: Did you resent it?

A: Very much. Especially since my wife had to tell me they
were cheating us.

Q: I see. Tell me, Mr. Montmorency, would you say your
resentment was such as to lead to the point of being desirous of
stuffing Mr. Carpenter through a porthole, or tossing him over-

board, if it came to that? Or, of course, doing harm to Mrs. Carpenter?

A: Easily. *(Minor sensation)*

Q: Let me understand you very clearly on this, Mr. Montmorency. Are you confessing to ridding this ship of the Carpenter family?

A: No. You asked if I would have liked to. I would have liked to. But I didn't.

Q: May I ask why not?

A: For the same reason I didn't knock your block off when the other fellows at the table told me *you* were cheating me.

Q: And that reason is?

A: My wife wouldn't let me.

Q: I see. I believe you can be excused, Mr. Montmorency. By the way, what do you weigh?

A: Twenty-one-odd stone. All muscle, if you want to check.

Q: Thank your wife for me, personally, will you? Thank you. May I have the next one in line, please? Ah, Mr. Wilkins, is it not?

A: It is. Jimmy Wilkins, bookmaker and not ashamed of it. None of this turf-banker nonsense for me!

Q: I assume that you, too, Mr. Wilkins, realized that the Carpenters were cheating you and that you did not require your wife to bring the fact to your attention?

A: You know something? I didn't for awhile. He was good, that bloke. Real good.

Q: I note you say "was," using the past tense. What makes you feel that Mr. Carpenter belongs in that particular time sequence?

A: Because someone done him in, didn't they? That's the way I heard it. I wouldn't speak of Zev in the present tense; nor Mrs. Carpenter, either, if it comes to that.

Q: I suppose you're right. To continue, though: how soon did you discover you were being cheated?

A: About the third rubber, I'd say. She wasn't anywhere near as cozy as him. And anyway, they were beating the odds just a bit much, if you know what I mean.

Q: I know exactly what you mean. But still, you continued to play?

A: Well, there wasn't any other game around, you see.

Q: There's always that, I suppose. Now, Mr. Wilkins, when you discovered you were being cheated, didn't it get you angry?

A: No, as a matter of fact. You see, when you're in my business, being cheated is all part of the bit, you might say. Everyone tries his hand at doing a bookmaker in the eye. It's sort of a game—can he get away with it or can't he? When I catch a bloke trying to cheat, I don't toss him and his account out into the gutter—my Lord, I'd be out of business in a week, if I did. I usually just tell him he didn't get away with it that time, and generally we end up with him buying me a pint and us having a good laugh about it over at the Hen and Eagle.

Q: Did you tell Mr. Carpenter he wasn't getting away with it? And did he end up standing you a pint and having a good laugh with you about it?

A: Well, no. First of all he was a Yank, and you know them and their sense of humor. Doesn't exist. And second, he never drank anything as far as I could see.

Q: Yes. . . . Well I suppose that's about all the questions I can think of as far as you're concerned, Mr. Wilkins. Thank you for your patience. Now, the next witness please? Ah! Mr. Tompkins, I believe . . .

A: That's right. Arthur Tompkins.

Q: A certified accountant, are you not?

A: That is correct.

Q: I find it difficult to believe that a man with your experience in numbers and percentages, etcetera, did not instantly discover that he was being cheated.

A: Well, I didn't. At least not in time, if that's what you mean. I'd lost a goodly sum before I was able to confirm my suspicions. As Mr. Wilkins testified before me, this Carpenter chap was good. He—

Q: Yes?

A: I was going to say, he was much better, incidentally, than you.

Q: Ah, well; one can't be the best in all things. But to return to the Carpenters; when did you discover you had been cheated?

A: About two hours after we were playing.

Q: And what did you do then?

A: Why, I stopped playing, of course!

Q: Did you notify the authorities?

A: Well—well, no. . . .

Q: May I ask why not?

A: Well . . .

Q: Let me put it to you this way, Mr. Tompkins: Mr. Montmorency is a man accustomed to handling matters of this nature without recourse to any authority other than himself. Mr. Jimmy Wilkins is a man accustomed by his profession to attempts to cheat him, and to maintaining silence regarding those attempts. But you, sir, are a certified accountant. As such you are trained to regard money as sacred. You are also well accustomed to call upon authority when normal respect for property rights regarding money is lacking, as it obviously is when one is being cheated. I find it difficult, therefore, to understand why you did not attempt to recover your losses through official channels, once you knew you were being cheated?

A: Er . . .

Q: Yes?

A: Well, if you must know, I took this cruise trip in order to handle some extremely confidential matters, and I didn't want any publicity to attach to my presence on the S.S. *Sunderland*—to come, that is, to the attention of my—ah—my competitors.

Q: Oh, ah! Sorry! Fortunately, it appears that the record of these proceedings may be somewhat less than complete, so I think you need have no worries on that score. You may be excused, Mr. Tompkins. Thank you. And the last of our card-playing witnesses? Mr. James Wellington?

A: The Reverend James Wellington, Sir Percival.

Q: I should have suspected. Well, I don't believe we need subject you to too many questions. You never did suspect you were being cheated, did you, Reverend?

A: I did not.

Q: Not even when Captain Manley-Norville came into the card room when I was out washing my hands and said that *I* was cheating you?

A: It wasn't the Captain. It was the library steward.

Q: And you still did not suspect?

A: I did not believe him.

Q: May I ask why not?

A: It would not have been charitable.

Q: Thank you! There are far too few left in this world with your pure mind, Reverend. May we play cards again together as soon as possible. You may be excused, and thank you very much. Hmmm! Well, that finishes our card-playing suspects. Let us now continue our search for the truth—may we have next the stewardess who was so unfortunate as to discover the body. Mrs. Penelope Watkins. Mrs. Watkins? If you'll just be seated, please?

"Why doesn't he have that slinky master-at-arms up for questioning?" Simpson asked in a low but perturbed tone of voice. He had managed seats beside himself for his newly released friends, and a steward was in the process of providing the trio with appropriate refreshment. "If I was putting this bash in a book, he's the chap I'd have on the carpet at this point!"

"Saving him for dessert," Briggs guessed, quite correctly. "Old Pugh likes to end a meal with a bang! He wants somebody he can make look guilty if he is or not, and that spiv King looks as guilty as that spiv steward who turned me in—"

"Who you didn't even see," Carruthers remarked.

Briggs paid no attention to the interruption. "Old Pugh needs somebody to start off the fall assizes with, and I guess old King James the Fifth is elected. Let's hope he has better luck than his namesake! Anyway, don't worry about old James V.—just worry about his savings account!"

"Hold it!" It was Carruthers, twisting about in his chair. A number of other passengers turned with him. "Here comes the doctor. Quick work, I must say! They must keep a live chicken in the laboratory for pregnancy tests, or something."

"You're thinking of rabbits," Briggs said. He grinned maliciously. "You'd best bone up on that sort of thing, Billy-boy, what with all the women that are going to be chasing you!"

Q: I'm very sorry, Mrs. Watkins, but I'm afraid I shall have to ask you to wait a few minutes. I see Doctor Ramsey has returned from his errand. We shall come to you in a few minutes. Thank you. And now, Doctor?

A: I did that test as you requested, Sir Percival.

Q: Ah! Fine! At a later point, Doctor, I shall explain to you just how I knew it was chicken blood, and just how the blood managed to get on the porthole sill.

A: I should be most interested to hear it, Sir Percival. Because there isn't the faintest doubt that the blood in that porthole sill is human blood. No doubt at all. . . . *(Sensation)*

14

"Well," said Sir Percival Pugh softly to nobody in the vicinity except himself. "Well, well, well." He considered his words and found them good. "Well!"

Captain Manley-Norville leaned over from his perch a bit anxiously.

"I say, Percy?"

"Yes?"

"What's all this chicken-blood thing?" He sounded puzzled, a rare thing with the Captain, and a state he didn't particularly enjoy. Captain Manley-Norville liked to know where everything was at any particular time and in which condition. "Don't tell me we have one of these voodoo cases on our hands?"

"No, it's not voodoo. It's simply that I was teeing off the wrong tee onto the wrong fairway. Other than that, I was coming in for a fair score, considering handicap."

"You?"

"Me. That's the handicap, this trip. Me. It comes, of course," he added evenly, "from listening to people and trustingly remembering what they told me."

"I say, Percy." Captain Manley-Norville lowered his voice even more. "How about dropping the whole thing? After all, you merely contracted to ease this Briggs chap and this Carruthers chap out of choky on E Deck, and you did that without raising a sweat. And," he added shrewdly, "you also did it in such a manner that they're almost bound to hare for home tomorrow from the Gibraltar airport by fastest means, leaving me in your debt for God knows how many bottles of bubbly. Which, of course, I consider a bargain."

Sir Percival smiled up at his friend.

"You're right on the button on all counts, Charles. As usual. Except that I can't very well drop it now. I'm just beginning to see light. Call it beginner's luck, but there it is."

"I have a tendency to call it a new client," Captain Manley-Norville said shrewdly. "How far off am I?"

"Two feet from the pin with no roll," Sir Percival conceded and smiled.

"But you want to get on with it?"

"If you haven't run out of vichy water."

Captain Manley-Norville smiled down from his platform. "Someday I'm going to bar you from this ship, Percy," he said in a half whisper and rapped on the music stand. Unfortunately he had forgotten to use the baton and he winced. "Court," he said in a voice that broke up the murmurs resounding throughout the room, "is in session."

"I wonder what old cutie-pie Pugh has under his hat right now," Briggs muttered suspiciously. "Look at that look on his face!"

"It's just possible if you keep quiet and listen you may find out," Carruthers suggested in a low voice and leaned back in his seat, trying not to be cognizant of the glances being sent his way by a large part of the feminine population—mostly above seventy—of the Main Salon. . . .

Q: Dr. Ramsey, thank you for your valuable information. I don't believe we need bother any further.

A: But you said—

Q: I say many things, and most of the things I've said here this evening can be classed as disregardable, if such a word exists. You may be excused, Doctor.

A: Well, all right, but I'd still like to know where you got the notion of chicken blood . . .

Q: Yes. Well, now, to return to you, Mrs. Watkins. You are the stewardess on B Deck?

A: Just the aft half, sir. Tilly Suffield, she handles the fore cabins.

Q: But you handle B-67?

A: Yes, sir.

Q: And, if the information furnished me by the purser is correct, a certain Alf Martin is the steward who works with you in your section?

A: That's right, sir.

Q: Good. Now, if you would be kind enough to tell us in your own words what happened on the noon of last Wednesday?

A: Well, sir, when I heard that some little old man all covered with perfume and lipstick was seen coming out of B-67, I figured something had to be fishy, because while I don't want to be catty, sir, this Mrs. Carpenter she just never struck me as being that kind. Not that I mean that as being complimentary, sir, though I don't mean that as being uncomplimentary either, sir. I'll admit she was a good-looking woman, if you like them all chest, but—while I don't like to speak ill of the dead, and like I said I don't want to be catty—she might have looked hot on the outside, but inside she was a cold potato. A woman can tell, sir, if you know what I mean.

Q: I suspect I do. Tell me, what about Mr. Carpenter? Was he what you would term a hot potato or a cold potato?

A: I couldn't rightly say, sir. I never seen him. He was always out of the cabin by the time I come on to clean up, but Mrs. Carpenter was a great one to sleep in when she could. But my guess, sir, is that Mr. Carpenter had to be a cold potato, too. I mean, to be married to a cold potato like his missus.

Q: Yes. Well, to return to the events we are investigating, you were saying?

A: Oh! About that Wednesday! Well, sir, when I heard about the old man coming out of the cabin and all that guff, I figured to meself, I says, Penny, old girl, I says, if something's missing from that stateroom, the old bit—biddy—who lives there, ten to one she'll accuse you of taking it, so you better check it out. And I did. I goes in there and looks all around, and it all looks okay to me, so I figures the steward was drunk, or giving me the needle or something, but I also figures that while I'm in there, I might as well check out the loo, because that's almost sort of automatic with us everytime we goes in a cabin, and I pulls back this shower curtain and—Gar! What a bleeding—I mean, what a mess!

Q: And then what happened?

A: Well, I guess I must have had the screaming meemies and the doctor come and the next thing I know I'm in the 'firmary and Mary, there, she's giving me a couple of pills and taking me to me cabin.

Q: Yes. However, if we could return to cabin B-67 for a moment, how is it that the steward—seeing a suspicious character emerging from the room—didn't investigate the matter himself? Why did he feel it necessary to suggest that you investigate?

A: Prolly because he didn't have a key, sir.

Q: Oh? Are stewardesses the lone guardians of the gate, so to speak? As I recall Mr. Williamson's testimony, I believe he stated that master keys were distributed with a more lavish hand than that. I believe he stated that master keys were in the possession of stewards, stewardesses, the master-at-arms, plus the Captain. Had I been misinformed?

A: Oh, no, sir. It's only that the master keys they issue to us stewards and stewardesses just fit the locks in our particular sections. Like mine: it fits all the cabins in B Decks aft, sir. It wouldn't fit any of Tilly's cabins, like, sir.

Q: I'm afraid you still have failed to clarify the matter in my mind. My question remains: How is it that Alf Martin didn't investigate this strange man coming out of B-67 himself?

A: Oh, this steward wasn't Alf, sir.

Q: I beg your pardon? Then who was he?

A: Now, sir, that's odd. Real odd. I mean, odd. Fifteen years I been on this bucket—begging your pardon, Captain—and I thought I knew them all, but this one was a new one, he was. I never seen him before in my life. He never pinched me, or anything like that, and I'd remember that, and almost every other steward—

Q: May I ask how you knew this man to be a steward, if you had never seen him before?

A: By his uniform, of course, sir. All the stewards wear white jackets and black bow ties, and us stewardesses, we wear white dresses and—but you must know all this, sir.

Q: I do. Tell me, Mrs. Watkins, how is it you are not wearing your glasses?

A: I don't wear them unless I have to, and I don't need them now, because—but land's sake, how did you ever know I even wear glasses, sir?

Q: A fortunate surmise, is all. I believe that will be all, Mrs. Watkins. Thank you.

CAPTAIN MANLEY-NORVILLE *(interrupting):* I say, Percy—I mean, Sir Percival—I'm not exactly sure what you're driving at, but I do know we have no new stewards on the roster. Certainly no steward so new that Mrs. Watkins would not recognize him, with or without her glasses.

SIR PERCIVAL: Should you be worried about an unidentified object on your payroll list, Captain, I wouldn't be if I were you. I believe what Mrs. Watkins saw and spoke to was a passenger.

CAPTAIN MANLEY-NORVILLE: A passenger? Wearing a steward's uniform?

SIR PERCIVAL: No, sir. A passenger wearing a passenger's uniform. His white dinner jacket and black tie.

CAPTAIN MANLEY-NORVILLE: At *noon*?

SIR PERCIVAL: Admittedly de trop, but I doubt if this particular passenger had gone to bed at all that Tuesday night. Certainly not in his own stateroom, or he would have put on something more comfortable for his disappearance.

CAPTAIN MANLEY-NORVILLE: You can only be referring to Mr. Carpenter.

SIR PERCIVAL: I only can, can't I? I might mention that should you decide to send the master-at-arms to conduct another search for the gentleman, that he be instructed to be a bit more thorough than he was on Tuesday night.

CAPTAIN MANLEY-NORVILLE: Master-at-arms! You will immediately take a group of sailors and search this ship again, do you hear? And I expect you to do a proper job this time, and look in every nook and cranny, do you understand? And don't come back until you bring Mr. Carpenter with you? Is that clear? *(Sensation)*

STATEMENT BY MR. MAXWELL CARPENTER:

I don't know why this Pugh character is trying to shut me up, because I'm sure not ashamed of what I did to Mazie, although I will admit people could find fault with me for taking so long to do it.

Mazie's trouble—did I say trouble? I mean one of her two thousand troubles—was that she was such a silly, bossy bitch. When she said jump, you weren't even allowed to ask her how high. And her card play? You'd think just watching me and

186

playing with me all these years would have taught her something, but not a prayer! Take her bridge. If I told her once I told her a thousand times you can't pick up a hand and open seven no-trump without even sorting out the cards—once, maybe, but certainly not six times in a row. Some jasper is bound to notice, I don't care how stupid he looks. And the only reason she didn't do something that dumb with those two old crooks was she didn't get a chance. I still would like to know how they got hold of every deck of cards on the ship.

Now you take that rape bit Mazie pulled. Just to get even! Good God! Only idiots do things to get even; only a purebred nut loses his temper. I wasn't angry when I killed Mazie. I admit I was a trifle irked, because she wouldn't even shut up when she was taking a shower, but I wasn't what you'd really call angry. I was just fed up with things all at once. Sending a posse out after me just because I wasn't in bed by midnight! You'd think I was ten years old!

I'd picked up a bottle of brandy someplace and I took it down to the gym—nobody's ever there at night; in fact, nobody's ever there during the day. They'd do better to make a card room out of it. Anyway, I never drink, and I guess this brandy conked me out. I was sitting on a pile of gym mats trying to figure out how to raise enough scratch to get back into a decent game, and the next thing I know I guess I fell asleep, because when I woke up and made it back to the cabin, it was already eight o'clock by my watch.

Anyway, I hammered on the door—she'd taken off the padlock to get in, of course, but she'd latched the thing from the inside—and I finally woke her up, and then she started in. She was even nastier than usual, which is something, believe me! And then I got a little irked, too, remembering that dumb chicken-swindle bit. I must have told her a dozen times since we were married that the chicken-swindle bit went out with the bustle—especially that dumb patter she insisted on using—and that on top of that, chicken blood tastes lousy. It also doesn't come out in cold water, and I was getting sick and tired of wearing shirts all spotted with little red dots. They don't look neat, and she knew how I liked to look neat. I must have told her a dozen times at least, but talk to the wall! A dozen times I told her tomato juice would do the trick just as well, but when Mazie got an idea in her pea brain, you couldn't budge it with a dock crane. It had to be chicken blood, she says, because she read it someplace. I wish people would be more careful what they write!

Anyway, she says since I already woke her up she's going to take a shower, but does that stop her from yammering? Don't bet on it! All it does is make her raise her voice. So I took off my jacket and shirt—it wasn't too clean, I'll admit, but it was the cleanest one I had—at least it didn't have spots of chicken blood all over it—and I picked up the knife from the fruit dish and I went in and I stuck her. And believe it or not, she kept talking nasty all the way down to the floor of the shower. That Mazie!

The knife? I tossed it out the porthole. It hit the sill and bounced, and for a minute I was afraid it was going to fall back inside right on my shirt, but it fell out into the water, which was luck. That's all I needed, my last shirt spotted too. I told her to send the others to the laundry, but like I said, talk to the wall!

Anyway, I was going to change, but then I figured they had to get around to cleaning the cabins pretty soon, so I just put on my shirt and grabbed the same jacket and beat it. I went up and hid in the lifeboat on the boat deck. But after an hour or so, I figured I'd come down and get some clean underwear and pick up that fruit while I was about it, but when I get down there here's this little character coming out of the cabin and pretending he's talking to Mazie. Well, I didn't know if it was just a trap or if the guy was nuts or what, but I figured I'd let the stewardess find out. I tipped her off and waited, but when she started to scream, I headed back to my lifeboat in a hurry, believe me!

Incidentally, Captain, about those lifeboats. Did you ever try to spend any time in one of them? Maybe for a boat drill they're all right—though I doubt it—but five minutes in the one I was in would have been too much, let alone since Wednesday morning. What day is it now, by the way? I sort of lost track. I'd sure hate to spend a month or two drifting all over the Atlantic in one of those wooden shoes in case this crate ever hit a floating beer case and went down. I think I broke a tooth on that rock they got marked hardtack, and when did they fill those water canisters? When they built this tub back in the First World War? And how much extra would it really have cost to put in a couple of bottles of booze? In case of sickness, say? I'm not much of a drinker, but at least booze doesn't get stale.

And would it have killed them to have upholstered those seats? Man, I've got calluses on top of calluses. . . .

STATEMENT BY SIR PERCIVAL PUGH:

It is tragic that my client—my new client, that is—was the victim of unfortunate circumstances in that he just happened to be holding a fruit knife in his hand while his loving wife was attempting to embrace him to show her appreciation for his efforts to fix her shower so she could enjoy her morning ablutions. Had he not made the attempt—and successfully—she might well have taken with pneumonia, for I'm sure you all recall my client's constant reference to cold water. I'm not sure if failure to maintain an adequate hot-water supply doesn't appear as malfeasance under Her Majesty's Regulations for the Operation of Seagoing Ships Flying the Union Jack, but you may be sure the matter will be investigated thoroughly and those responsible brought to justice!

189

Did I hear someone in the audience ask, what about his confession?

What confession?

Surely you intelligent ladies and gentlemen will not be misled by the hysterical words of a poor chap forced to undergo the deprivation of drinking only water for a period of several days, nor by his suffering the pangs of toothache due to our lifeboats being supplied with the stalest of provender undoubtedly at the behest of company directors seeking only profit rather than caring about the comfort of the passengers in their charge. The Captain and I have been friends for many years, but friendship cannot be used to avoid official responsibility where—not only a man's freedom, but his comforts, as well—are concerned. Just think, ladies and gentlemen, in case of an emergency *you* might have been the one to discover the brackish nature of the water and the indurate nature of the buns.

Confession, forsooth! The tormented words of a man who has been made to sleep on the rigid seat of a lifeboat designed with no thought of anything except the cheapest way to prevent the ship line from facing insurance claims!

Confession, indeed! Ah, no, ladies and gentlemen! Under far less pressure have stronger men quailed, broken, muttered the first foolish falsehood that came to their benumbed brain. A few days' rest under my care and I am sure that the truth shall emerge. Rather than condemn, we should applaud. Mr. Maxwell Carpenter had the great satisfaction of knowing his wife died in comfort, due to his ministrations to the plumbing of her shower. Her last earthly feelings had to be of warmth; the warmth of the water her husband had arranged, the warmth of his affection—nay, love—for her; the warmth of happiness.

How many of us, tragically and inadvertently causing the death of a dear one through an unfortunate accident such as occurred in this case, can say we have left our loved one in such comfort . . . ?

190

*(Unbridled applause by the audience, led
by none other than James V. King, master-at-arms, who was seen to unashamedly
brush aside a tear.)*

STATEMENT BY CAPTAIN CHARLES EVERTON
MANLEY-NORVILLE *(in an aside to his old
friend Sir Percival Pugh):*

I imagine you'll be getting off at Gibraltar with the prisoner,
Percy. Don't come back.

STATEMENT BY MR. TIMOTHY BRIGGS *(as he
and his companions carry their own luggage down the gangplank at Gibraltar):*

Next time maybe you bright lads will pay some attention to
me. I tried to tell you all along that we should have our eyes
peeled for that spiv steward who turned me in. . . .